FOLLOW THE CODES . . .

Join Art and Camille in viewing famous art with the interactive QR codes feature you'll discover in these pages.

To access the images you will need a smartphone or tablet and a connection to the Internet. If you don't have a QR reader app on your device, ask a parent or guardian to download a free QR reader from the app store. Once you have downloaded the app, simply open it and hover the device over the QR code, which looks like this:

The art will appear in your browser.

The QR codes simply provide a link to the website of a museum or library or a location of historical significance. If you don't have access to a QR reader or if a link expires, be sure to visit the websites directly to learn more about the artwork and locations mentioned in the book. The museums, libraries, and locations include the British Museum, St George's Chapel at Windsor Castle, the National Gallery (UK), the National Portrait Gallery (UK), the Yale Center for British Art, the Royal Collection Trust, and the University of Michigan Library. Happy sleuthing!

The Crown HEIST

The Crown HEIST

DERON HICKS

A LOST ART MYSTERY

CLARION BOOKS

An Imprint of HarperCollins*Publishers*

BOSTON   NEW YORK

Clarion Books is an imprint of HarperCollins Publishers.

The Crown Heist
Copyright © 2021 by Deron Hicks
Map copyright © 2021 by Ute Simon

clarionbooks.com

The Library of Congress Cataloging-in-Publication Data is on file.
ISBN: 978-0-358-39606-2

The text was set in Weiss.
Cover design by Alice Wang
Interior design by Alice Wang

Manufactured in the United States of America
1 2021
4500836203

First Edition

*To Margaret Anna Hicks (Mercer University, class of 2020),
Miles Parker Hicks (Brookstone School, class of 2020), and all
of their classmates. And in memory of Murphy.*

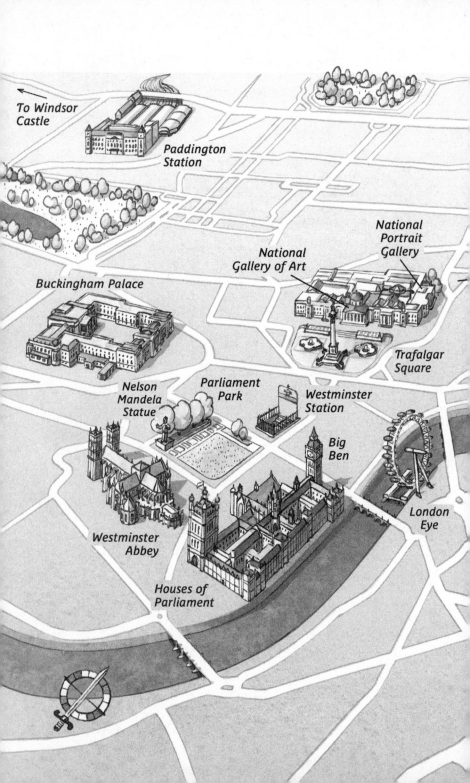

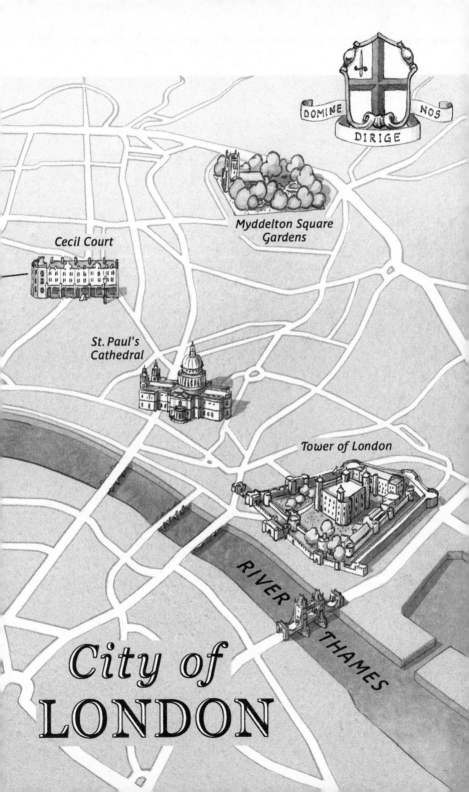

DOMINE DIRIGE NOS

Myddelton Square
Gardens

Cecil Court

St. Paul's
Cathedral

Tower of London

RIVER THAMES

City of
LONDON

The aim of art is to represent not the
outward appearance of things, but
their inward significance.

—Aristotle

PROLOGUE

6:12 a.m.
Two years ago
Yale Center for British Art, Yale University
New Haven, Connecticut

Samuel Gamble took one last sip of coffee and then placed his heavy stoneware cup on the credenza in his office.

It was time to walk.

Today was the opening of a new exhibit, and—as always—Gamble was a bundle of nerves. He had spent the previous three days overseeing the final preparations—rereading the pamphlets and the exhibit catalog, checking the signage and labels, working with consultants, adjusting the lighting, reviewing security precautions, and, for what seemed like the millionth time, making sure that every single item in the exhibit was arranged exactly, precisely, as it should be.

Gamble had served as the director of the Yale Center for British Art for more than ten years, and for every single day of those ten years he had been the first person to arrive at the center each morning. It was a habit he had learned from his father, a high school principal. He followed the same route through the center each morning. The path never varied, even on days such as this. It was important, Gamble believed, to maintain a routine — to be consistent. It allowed him to calm down and prepare for the day. He loved walking the halls and floors of the center before any of the other staff had arrived. He loved the echo of his feet as he made his way around the empty building, through artwork from the past five hundred years — from antiquity to the twenty-first century. He loved the solitude.

Gamble made his way out of his office and through a broad entrance hall filled with sculptures. The new exhibit was located two floors above him. And despite a desperate desire to rush immediately to the exhibit — to check every detail once again — he told himself to be patient.

Follow the routine.

Hanging above the welcome desk was a large banner. Gamble paused ever so briefly to admire it. The banner read:

TIME FOR ENGLAND: THE EXHIBIT

AUGUST 15–SEPTEMBER 21

YALE CENTER FOR BRITISH ART

THIRD FLOOR

A smile creased Gamble's face. He was confident that his guests would be pleased.

Gamble continued his route through the entrance lobby. Small signs strategically placed throughout the first floor gently guided visitors toward the stairs and elevator leading to the exhibit. All seemed to be in order.

Despite the availability of an elevator, he made his way up the wide concrete and granite stairs to the second floor.

As he walked, Gamble ran through the details of the exhibit in his head. The exhibit explored the concept of time in British art and history — how time had been measured, discussed, written about, and expressed in art over the centuries. A number of very important academics had been invited to attend the opening that morning, and Gamble was also expecting numerous reporters. It had taken years of negotiations and discussions with libraries and museums across the world to bring the exhibit together, and representatives from all of the museums and libraries would also be present.

Gamble reached the second floor and made his way around the stairs, past the reference library, and through the rare-books room. He then passed through the small foyer and into the collection space. Gamble paused briefly to admire a large painting by the eighteenth-century painter Edward Edwards. It was a painting of the interior of Westminster Abbey, the massive church in the center of London. The painter had captured the inside of the church in astonishing detail. Gamble had visited the abbey frequently as a youth growing up on the outskirts of London. And even though more than two hundred years separated his fond memories of the abbey from those rendered in paint by Edward

Edwards, the church had changed very little in appearance.

Gamble continued patiently through and around the second-floor collection and soon found himself standing at the stairway leading to the third floor.

This is it, he thought.

He took a deep breath and made his way up to the landing between the floors. This was the first view that visitors would have of the exhibit. It had to be perfect. It had to capture everything that the exhibit was intended to be. A visitor's eyes would be immediately drawn to the large sign. Printed in black and white, it read simply TIME. He had spent a week adjusting the lighting to ensure that the sign could be seen from every angle without unnecessary shadows or reflections.

Gamble smiled.

The sign *was* perfect.

Visitors would be impressed.

He made his way slowly up the stairs toward the third floor. As he ascended, he allowed his eyes to drift slowly down from the sign to a glass exhibition case on the far side of the foyer. It was the first display that visitors would see as they entered the third floor. It held only one object—the symbol of the exhibit. It would serve as just a hint of what was to come—a crowning achievement. It would . . .

Gamble gasped.

No.

No, no, no, no.

He sprinted up the stairs and across the foyer.

Moments later Gamble found himself standing directly in front of the display case.

He couldn't believe what he was seeing.

It was gone.

CHAPTER 1

3:00 p.m.
Tuesday, August 12
Washington, DC

"Nervous?" Art asked. Art and Camille sat on the stoop outside Camille's home waiting for her mother to complete a work call before they headed to the airport. It would be Camille's first overseas flight.

Camille nodded but said nothing, which was out of character.

Art, on the other hand, did not feel the least bit nervous about getting on the plane. He was a seasoned traveler despite having only recently turned thirteen. He had spent countless hours on planes crisscrossing the globe as he tagged along with his father, Arthur Hamilton Sr. Art's dad —Dr. Hamilton, as he was known to his colleagues—was one of the top art conservation scientists on the planet. He had spent a good portion of his life—and practically all of Art's life—traveling from museum to museum to supervise, assist, and direct the preservation of some of the most important works of art in the world. That nomadic life had changed this past year when Dr. Hamilton had assumed the

7

position as head of conservation at the Lunder Center at the National Portrait Gallery in Washington, DC. Their travels for the past several months had been largely confined to the local coffee shop and bookstore, which suited Art just fine. It was nice to go home to the same bedroom each night. He could actually put a print up on his wall for the first time in his life — a replica of the original *Star Wars* movie poster. He had not been able to do that in any of the hotels and short-term apartments that they had lived in over the previous twelve years.

But now Art found himself once more preparing for a transatlantic flight. And for the first time in his life he was traveling without his father, who was going to remain in Washington, DC. The reason for this particular trip was the person sitting next to him: Camille Sullivan. Camille was his best friend, and she had asked if he would come with her to London. Art knew that Camille had a good reason for being nervous — and not just because this was her first flight over the Atlantic Ocean. Camille was twelve years old. And in those twelve years, she had never met her father. That would change once they landed.

"It will be okay," Art assured her.

"Mom said that I shouldn't get too excited about meeting my dad," Camille replied. "I think she's afraid I'll be disappointed."

Camille pulled a small necklace from beneath her shirt and showed it to Art. Hanging from the thin gold chain was a dark gray rectangular object. Tiny symbols and letters covered the surface of the stone.

"My dad sent me this last week," she said. "I try to keep it hidden. I know my mom's not real happy about all of this."

Art recognized the object instantly. It was a miniature copy of the Rosetta Stone—one of the most important archeological discoveries in history. The inscriptions on the stone, which dated back more than two thousand years, had allowed archeologists to unlock the secrets of Egyptian hieroglyphs—the lost language of the ancient Egyptians.

"Your mom's taking you to London to meet your father," Art replied. "That's something."

And it *was* something. Camille's father had left her mother before Camille was born, and now he suddenly wanted to be part of Camille's life. Camille's mother had every reason not to trust his motives.

"I suppose," Camille said as she slipped the necklace back under her shirt. "What if he doesn't like me?"

"Not a chance," Art said.

Camille did not immediately respond.

"Thanks for coming," she finally replied.

Art patted Camille on her arm. She was his best friend, and they had been through a lot in the time they'd known each other. They had rescued his father from a group of art forgers and had managed to prevent the largest art theft in history. They had been threatened, chased, and tied up. They had even met the Queen of England. And through it all, Camille had been Camille—brash, smart, and fearless. All of that seemed to have vanished as they were waiting on the stoop. His friend was scared. He needed to be there for her.

"It will be okay," he repeated.

It was all he could say.

CHAPTER 2

8:00 p.m.
Tuesday, August 12
Main Library, University College London
London, England

The security guard tipped his hat. "Have a good night, Professor Tinsley."

"Same to you, Tom," Broderick Tinsley replied.

Broderick made his way out of the main library and down the marble steps to the plaza in front of the massive stone building. As a history professor at University College London, he was a virtual fixture at the library, known to most of the staff on a first-name basis.

It was a beautiful summer evening—warm, a slight breeze, and clear skies. Broderick stopped at the bottom of the steps to enjoy the last remnants of the day's sunlight on his face. He removed a cap from his satchel—a well-worn, baggy green cricket cap—and pulled it down over his rapidly graying red hair.

Broderick checked his watch. He was scheduled to meet his daughter at Heathrow Airport at eight o'clock the following morning. And despite telling himself that everything would be fine, he could feel his nerves bubbling just below the surface. His daughter had every reason to hate his guts. He had literally abandoned his pregnant wife just prior to Camille's birth. At the time he had had all sorts of justifications for doing so. He had never wanted children—he had seen them as an impediment to his career as a professor of history. His was a life of travel, research, and writing—a life dedicated to teaching.

What role did a child play in that?

None whatsoever.

And so he had simply left it all behind.

And everything had gone great. He had eventually obtained a job teaching. He had written a number of highly respected books on the history of England. His lectures were in great demand. He had a wonderful home filled with books and antiques.

His life had been a resounding success.

His ex-wife and the daughter he had never met were long forgotten parts of his past.

He had had no regrets. None whatsoever.

And then four months ago, he saw a picture in the news of a red-haired young girl who had helped stop the largest art theft in history. He didn't even need to read the caption to know who the girl was. He recognized her instantly although he had never seen her in his entire life.

It was Camille.

It was his daughter.

He had run his finger over the picture. There she was

—a head full of red hair and a big toothy grin. It was as if he were looking at a picture of himself as a child.

"What have I done?" he had asked himself.

In an instant, his whole world came crashing down. He couldn't sleep. He couldn't focus on his lectures. Emails went unanswered. Phone calls were unreturned. Maybe it had been guilt—if so, it was certainly warranted. And so he had written his ex-wife a letter. He had not offered any excuses—just an apology for being so stupid and a simple request to meet his daughter.

Two weeks passed without a response. Broderick had been disappointed but not surprised. Camille and her mother had every right to be angry with him. His daughter had every right to ignore him for the rest of his life. But then —just when he had convinced himself that Camille had washed her hands of him—an email arrived. It was from Mary Sullivan, Camille's mother. She provided an email address for Camille and a suggestion that he send her an email. Mary Sullivan had said it would be up to Camille to decide whether she wanted to respond. He had sent the email, and Camille had responded. And now, after a month of emails, letters, Skype sessions, and phone calls, he was finally going to meet his daughter in person.

GURRGLE GURRGLE.

The noise from Broderick's stomach was loud enough to catch the attention of a couple of students standing to his right.

"Sorry 'bout that," Broderick said.

As usual, Broderick had skipped dinner—and his stomach was tired of being ignored. It had been growling at him for the past half hour. Fortunately, there was a small coffee stand just around the corner that served the most delicious Cornish pasties. Broderick smiled. A cup of coffee and a warm pasty would hit the spot, and it might help settle his nerves.

Broderick purchased his coffee and pasty and then made his way over to a small park directly behind the library. He located a bench beneath an elm tree and settled in with his late snack. He had started to take a bite from his pasty when he noticed a tall, heavily muscled man standing directly in front of him. The man was bald and had a thick mustache. He held a cup of coffee in one hand and a large brown envelope in the other.

"May I join you?" the man asked. His voice was deep. An American, most likely, but the accent was strangely indistinct.

Broderick glanced around the park. There were several empty benches.

Had the man mistaken him for someone else?

Maybe he liked the view of the park from this particular bench?

"Uh, sure," Broderick finally blurted out. "I won't be much longer."

The man sat down on the other side of the bench.

"No need to rush away," he said. "Besides, I came here to see you."

"Me?" Broderick asked. He had never seen the man before in his life.

"Yes," the man replied. "You are Broderick Tinsley, correct?"

Broderick nodded.

"The same Broderick Tinsley who serves as a professor of history at University College London?"

Broderick nodded once more.

The man smiled. "Excellent," he said as he slid the brown envelope across the bench to Broderick. "Then I believe, Professor Tinsley, that you will find this very interesting."

CHAPTER 3

6:05 a.m.
Wednesday, August 13
Somewhere over the North Atlantic

Art yawned and stretched his arms high over his head. He had been asleep for almost five hours. He glanced over at Camille, who sat in the seat next to him on the airplane.

"You're awake," Camille said, her legs crossed and her head tethered to the armrest by a pair of ear buds. The movie *Captain Marvel* played silently on the small screen opposite her seat. Her hair—curly and generally unruly—had been pulled back and tied into place with a black scrunchie. Art could tell by the tone in her voice that whatever nerves she may have had before getting on the plane had vanished.

"I don't see how you can sleep on a plane," she added as she removed her ear buds. "I can't seem to get comfortable."

A constant stream of caffeine and sugar will do that to you, Art thought, noting the three cans of Coke sitting on Camille's service tray.

"Did you get any sleep?" he asked.

Camille shook her head. "Not really," she replied. "Too excited."

Camille had been talking nonstop about meeting her father for the past two weeks—ever since her mother had agreed to take her to London to visit him. But Art also knew that she would be absolutely exhausted once they arrived at the airport. After all, she had not slept for almost twenty-four hours.

"Thanks for coming along," she added.

"Not a problem," replied Art. And it wasn't a problem at all. He loved London. The city had been around for almost two thousand years, a fact that always amazed him. It had survived plagues, fires, and war. There was history everywhere. And, to Art's great delight, London also happened to have some of the best art museums in the world—the National Gallery, the National Portrait Gallery, Tate Modern. And those museums housed some of the most famous paintings in the world —works by van Gogh, Rembrandt, Monet, and Picasso. His particular favorite was a panel by Leonardo da Vinci, one of the few completed paintings by the master in existence. It was breathtaking in its detail, its depth of color, and its naturalism. Art absolutely adored London. But there was something more—something he did not want to admit to Camille. The more he read about Camille's father, the more intrigued Art became. Professor Broderick Tinsley had written extensively on the history of England, with a particular emphasis on the Renaissance period. He was not simply an academic who spent all his time locked away in some library. To the contrary, Professor Tinsley was considered an adventurer of sorts. He didn't just write and teach about history, he was constantly out looking for it—roaming the British Isles to find important pieces of the past, wherever those pieces might be located. Art had watched several videos of Professor Tinsley's lectures and speeches. His stories were fascinating. But Art also understood that it was this very part of Professor Tinsley that had led him to abandon his wife and yet-to-be-born daughter all those years ago. Professor Tinsley chased history and fame while Camille's mother raised a child. That made Art feel guilty about wanting to meet Camille's father. And despite knowing how excited Camille was to see her father, Art also understood how painful it had been for Camille over the years—something she had not admitted to anyone other than Art.

A voice announced over the intercom that the breakfast service was starting.

Good, Art thought. He was famished, and they still had a full day ahead of them.

He looked over at Camille, who had turned her attention back to *Captain Marvel.* A slight smile creased his face.

He was happy for his friend.

In just a few hours she would get to meet her father for the very first time.

"Brilliant," said Broderick Tinsley. "Absolutely brilliant."

Miles Davenport towered behind Broderick as Broderick held the ancient object under the lamp on his desk. They stared down at the delicate script that had appeared as if by magic. Despite the circumstances, Broderick could not help but be impressed.

"Now the hard work begins," said Broderick. He took several pictures of the script with his cell phone.

"Don't waste time taking pictures of it," Davenport said. "We'll just take the whole thing with us."

"Not a chance," Broderick replied. "If we got caught with this, we would have a lot of explaining to do."

Broderick knew he was right. They didn't need any unnecessary complications. And besides, the photos would provide everything they needed.

"But what do we do with it?" Davenport asked. "Just toss it in the river?"

A look of horror crossed Broderick Tinsley's face. "Throw it in the river?" he said. "Are you mad?"

Then he collected himself. "Don't worry," he finally told Davenport. "It will be perfectly safe until we return."

CHAPTER 4

9:35 a.m.

Wednesday, August 13

London, England

It was stupid.

She knew it was stupid.

But she couldn't help herself.

During the ride from Victoria station to their hotel, Camille had anxiously scanned the crowds of pedestrians and stared at the drivers of the other cars and their passengers. She had closely examined the faces in the windows of the buses as they passed.

Maybe, just maybe, she would see him. There was always a chance. Maybe.

Her father had not been at the airport when they had landed, but sometimes things happen.

Maybe his car had broken down.

Maybe he had gotten sick.

So they had tried his cell phone. No answer.

And then they had called his office at the college. An administrative assistant told her mother that her father would be gone for a week—maybe longer. A "sudden emergency" was how her father had described it to his assistant.

Sudden emergency.

"He's not coming, is he?" Camille had asked her mother at the airport.

Her mother shook her head. "No," she replied. "He's not."

Mary Sullivan did not seem very surprised by the turn of events, just angry.

Camille did her best to hold in the tears. She didn't want to make a spectacle of herself in the middle of a crowded airport. So she had held on to the only thing she had—hope.

Maybe something had happened.

Maybe her mother was wrong.

Although Camille had never met her father in person, she had committed his face to memory. They had Skyped several times. And there were the YouTube videos—dozens of his lectures were online. She knew that he spoke with an English accent, that he stood just over six feet tall, and that he favored blue jeans and sweaters. He had red hair that was quickly turning gray. She would recognize him anywhere.

But what would she do if she did see him?

Would she leap from the taxi and chase him down?

Would she grab him and demand answers, or simply hug him?

It was just plain stupid.

But she couldn't stop staring.

The taxi made its final turn and pulled up in front of their hotel. Camille took her bag from the taxi driver and hurried toward the front door to get out of the light mist of rain that had started to fall.

CHAPTER 5

11:13 a.m.
Wednesday, August 13
The Dorchester Hotel
London, England

He had lived off coffee for the past fifteen hours. A fresh pot was already brewing to get him through the day.

The thick curtains had been drawn shut, and a small desk lamp and the illumination from his tablet were the only lights in the room. Books, journals, and notepads covered the small hotel desk, most of the floor, and every chair in the room. He had turned off his cell phone to avoid the relentless barrage of emails, text messages, and calls. He was exhausted and had a headache that would not go away.

The bubbling sound of the coffee machine stopped. The coffee was ready. He poured himself a large cup and returned to the desk.

He wrote the words again: "weak field."

And again: "weak field."

And again, and again, and again—as if by sheer repetition the answer might arrive.

Broderick crumpled up the sheet in frustration and

threw it into the corner of the room, where it joined hundreds of other crumpled pieces of paper.

He was no closer to where he needed to be. And he was running out of time.

Broderick took a large gulp of the steaming hot coffee. It burned the back of his throat, but it was just the jolt he needed.

He had promised Davenport he could do this.

And he would.

It had been hidden for centuries in plain view. No one had understood or appreciated its true importance.

He had to give Davenport credit.

The man had unearthed an ancient document that suggested it was more than it appeared, and Davenport's hunch had been correct.

But the words now mocked Broderick.

Weak field.

Broderick was exhausted. His thoughts were all over the place, and the words were beginning to get jumbled up in his head.

Broderick paused.

Jumbled.

He sat up straight in his chair and looked at the pile of papers in the corner of the room.

Of course, he thought.

Broderick pulled out another pad of paper and started

scribbling furiously. One sheet of paper after another was discarded in rapid succession. And then, finally, everything fell into place.

It was . . . unbelievable.

Broderick turned on his cell phone and typed out a quick message to Miles Davenport.

"Problem solved," he wrote. "But we now have a new one."

CHAPTER 6

1:45 p.m.
Wednesday, August 13
London, England

Camille lay in the bed in her hotel room and stared at the ceiling. Her mother had offered to send her and Art on a tour of the city—something to get her mind off the fact that her father had, once again, disappeared from her life. But Camille had no interest in riding around in a double-decker bus while some tour guide pointed at every historical nook and cranny in the city of London. Under normal circumstances, that might have been interesting—maybe. But these were not normal circumstances.

Her mother, who was clearly angry over the morning's events, did not push the issue. If Camille wanted to sit in the hotel room and stare at the ceiling, Mary Sullivan was completely okay with letting her daughter do exactly that. Besides, Mary had arranged three days' worth of business meetings in London, all under the assumption that Camille and Art would spend the time visiting with Camille's father. Those meetings could not be postponed, so Mary Sullivan had headed off to her first meeting shortly after they had settled into the hotel earlier that morning.

Camille had spent most of the day lying in bed, watching television and feeling sorry for herself. Art had checked in on her occasionally and brought her a sandwich for lunch. He even offered to hang out with her and keep her company, but she just wanted to be alone. She continued to call and text her father's cell phone throughout the day, all to no avail. She kept telling herself that she needed to get angry at him, but that persistent flicker of hope continued to hang around.

Her mother did not trust her father and had warned Camille before the trip not to get too excited. But it had been a useless exercise. Camille *had* been excited. She had gone to bed each evening for the past two weeks thinking of what it would be like to meet her father in person. They had planned to visit all the sights in London and go on a day trip to see Stonehenge. She had thought of a million questions that she wanted to ask him. They had even planned to have dinner at his house this evening. He had promised to cook her favorite . . .

Camille sat upright in the bed.

His house.

She hopped off the bed, grabbed her backpack, and threw it open, rummaging around inside. She pulled out a small stack of papers with a rubber band wrapped around them. They were the letters her father had sent her over the past month. They were handwritten, not typed. There was very little in the letters that was not said on the phone, on Skype, in the text messages, or in the emails. But the way those same words were written—in her father's tight, neat script—made everything seem so much more real and personal.

She removed the rubber band from the letters and pulled one out. On the front of the envelope was her address in Washington, DC. And in the top left corner was her father's address in London. Mary Sullivan had selected the hotel in which they were staying because it was reasonably close to her father's home. Camille quickly typed the address into the map app on her phone. The location immediately appeared on the screen, and Camille hit "Directions." A moment later the map broadened out and a red line appeared between the location of the hotel and her father's home.

It was fewer than three blocks away.

Camille tapped out a quick text to Art.

CHAPTER 7

This is such a bad idea, Art thought.

Camille checked the directions on her phone. They were now less than a block away from her father's home.

"This way," she said. She pointed at the small blue and white road sign on the side of the building to their right that read MYDDELTON PASSAGE. They turned down the narrow tree-lined lane. To their left a tall brick wall ran the length of the roadway, and to their right was a long row of town homes. A well-maintained hedgerow guarded the front of the townhouses.

Camille's text message—sent less than half an hour ago—had caught Art off-guard. Art had asked what she expected to find when she got there. Camille didn't have an answer. She just said that she needed to see it.

But that wasn't what worried Art.

What if her father *was* there?

What if he wasn't away on some sudden trip?

What if he had simply been ignoring all of Camille's text messages and calls?

But Camille had insisted that she needed to see her father's home, and Art wasn't about to let her venture forth alone into a city she had never visited.

"We're here," Camille said.

They came to a stop in front of a set of stairs leading to a door that had been painted royal blue. A brass plaque to the right of the door identified it as NO. 4 MYDDELTON PASSAGE.

This is such a bad idea, Art thought once more.

Camille pulled the envelope from her pocket and checked the address.

No. 4 Myddelton Passage.

This was the right place.

The town home was narrow, three stories tall, and built of brick and stone. There was a large window to the right of the door, but thick drapes kept her from seeing inside.

She could feel her heart beating furiously in her chest. Part of her wanted to simply turn around and head back to the hotel. It would be easier that way—spend a couple of days sightseeing in London and then hop on a plane back to the States. There was no need to pursue her father. He had rejected her again. Why bother giving him yet another chance to break her heart? She should just put all of this behind her and be done with it.

But I have to do this, she told herself.

Camille took a deep breath and started up the steps. Art followed close behind.

A large brass knocker was attached to the middle of the door. Camille reached out and placed her hand on it.

"Are you sure about this?" Art asked.

Camille nodded. Her mouth had suddenly gone dry.

She lifted the knocker and let it drop. It landed with a loud clank on the thick brass plate to which it was attached. The sound echoed down the narrow lane. She repeated the process twice more, and then she stepped back from the door to wait.

Camille held her breath and listened for any sound from within the house.

Nothing.

She stood and stared at the door for what seemed like an eternity. Her heart felt as if it were going to explode from her chest.

Why did I do this? she asked herself.

She felt foolish.

"No one's here," she said to Art as she turned to go. It was time to return to the hotel. It was time to get back to reality.

But Art didn't move.

"Let's go," Camille said. "Nobody's—"

"Listen," Art interrupted.

"Listen to what?" Camille asked. But as soon as the words had left her mouth, she heard it. It was unmistakable.

It was the sound of footsteps.

Someone was approaching the front door.

CHAPTER 8

2:17 p.m.
Wednesday, August 13
London, England

Camille's heart—beating so furiously just a moment before —seemed to have come to a complete stop, and her breath held itself in her lungs. The sound of the footsteps grew closer and closer.

She glanced over at Art. Normally he was the absolute picture of calm. Nothing seemed to rattle him. But it was clear that the sound of footsteps on the far side of the blue door had taken him by surprise as well.

The footsteps came to a sudden stop.

There was a slight pause, and Camille wondered if she had been mistaken. Sounds had a way of fooling people. Maybe it was someone walking around in the home next door. The town homes shared common walls, so—Camille surmised—that was a possibility. Or perhaps the sound was an old pipe. Camille knew that old pipes sometimes made knocking sounds, and her father's townhouse was certainly old enough to have those types of pipes. Maybe that was what was happening.

But then she heard the distinct click of the bolt in the lock. There was no mistaking that sound. Someone was unlocking the door.

Camille's heart immediately jumped back into high gear. The door began to creak open.

Camille could feel all the blood rushing to her face.

What do I say?

What do I do?

Once more the urge to simply turn around and leave seized hold of her, and it took every ounce of courage to keep her feet planted firmly in place on the steps. Camille held her breath in anticipation.

The door suddenly swung open, and standing in the entryway was . . . a short woman with dark brown hair that had been pulled back into a bun. A pair of thick-framed glasses sat on top of her head. She wore a dark blue skirt and —despite the temperature outside hovering around eighty degrees—a gray sweater.

"Can I help you?" the woman asked. Her tone was polite but formal. She reminded Camille of the principal at her school back in Washington, DC.

Camille had no idea what to say. Had they come to the wrong house? Who was this woman?

But before Camille could answer, the woman's eyes went wide. She plucked the glasses from atop her hair and put them on. "Ahh," she said. "You are . . . Wait, don't tell me, I know this. You're Camille, right?"

The woman smiled and extended her hand to Camille. "I'm Costello Masters," she said. "My friends call me Cos. I'm a colleague of your father's. He asked me to stop by and take care of a few errands for him while he was gone."

Camille took the woman's hand and shook it. "It's nice to meet you," she said. "But how do you know who I am?"

The woman grinned. "Because your dad never shuts up about you," she said. "And, quite frankly, you are the spitting image of him — red hair and all."

The woman's statement caught Camille completely off-guard. It had never occurred to her that she actually looked like her father. It somehow made everything both better and worse at the same time.

Cos Masters continued to stare at Camille in the expectation of some sort of response. Art needed to do something. He stepped forward and extended his hand to the woman.

"My name's Art," he said. "I'm Camille's friend. We were just . . . well . . . checking to see if Professor Tinsley had returned home yet. We were supposed to meet him this morning."

Cos Masters shook her head. "I am afraid not," she replied. "His text message last night said that he would be gone a week, perhaps longer. He didn't give a lot of details. But it must have been terribly important for him to have rushed off so quickly. He asked me to stop by and check on Sherlock."

"Sherlock?" asked Camille. The last bit of news seemed to jar Camille out of her stunned state.

"Yes," Cos Masters replied. "Your father's pet bird. Some sort of parrot that he named Sherlock. He taught it to speak Latin — can you imagine that? I'll be honest, I can't stand the bird. My Latin is terrible, and I'm pretty sure the bird insults me every time I step into the room. But someone has to feed it — so, again, here I am. Unfortunately, your father is almost completely out of bird food. I was about to pop down to the grocery store for a new bag when you knocked."

The woman paused. She seemed to recognize how hard this was for Camille.

"Do you want to hang out here while I'm gone?" Cos Masters asked. "I shouldn't be more than ten or fifteen minutes. I mean . . . if you want to?"

Art glanced over at Camille. This was another bad idea. Nothing good could come of this. All it would do was cause his friend more pain. But he also knew that there was no way he was going to be able to talk her out of this.

"Yes," Camille replied. "I would like to do that."

CHAPTER 9

2:19 p.m.
Wednesday, August 13
London, England

They stood in the doorway of her father's house and watched as Cos Masters made her way down the lane, rounded the corner, and disappeared. Art knew how hard this was for Camille. Her father's phone was obviously working—he had, after all, sent a text message to Cos Masters the previous day asking her to take care of his parrot. The fact that he had not communicated at all with his daughter had to be eating at Camille. But it also felt somewhat creepy going into the home of someone whom Art did not know at all and whom Camille had never actually met. The truth was that Camille didn't really know her father. The emails, texts, and phone conversations had all been carefully controlled environments. This was not. Her father's home was a glimpse into who he really was, and that concerned Art. Camille might not like what she found.

"We don't have to go inside," Art said. "We could just stay here and wait until she gets back."

But Camille had already turned and headed into her father's house.

Art sighed and followed her inside.

They found themselves standing in a long hallway. Two amber globe lamps hung from the high ceiling and provided the only light in the narrow corridor. A set of dark wooden stairs at the end of the hallway disappeared into the floors above them. And despite his feeling that entering the home was a mistake, Art had to work hard to suppress a smile. It was exactly how Art had imagined the home of Professor Broderick Tinsley would be. Practically every inch of the wall in the hallway was covered with something—small paintings and prints, a couple of brightly colored Tibetan masks, a concert poster for a band named King Harvest, framed letters, box frames filled with insects, and hundreds of sepia-colored photographs. Stacks of books and magazines lined the wall. It was a complete, random mess—and it was wonderful.

"What now?" Art asked. During the course of their various escapades, it was a question that Camille had frequently asked him.

Camille shrugged. "This way," she said as she ventured down the hallway.

They passed a doorway to their right that led to a small parlor at the front of the house. It was—relatively speaking—far less of a mess than the hallway, a space obviously used by Camille's father to entertain guests. Camille glanced inside.

"No," she muttered, and then continued on down the hallway.

They passed another doorway, which led into a small dining room. Once more, Camille glanced briefly inside. She shook her head.

"No," she muttered again.

They reached a third doorway, just before the stairs leading to the second floor. Camille flipped on the light switch. It was the kitchen. It smelled of garlic and coffee. The floor was black and white tile in a checkerboard pattern, and the cabinets were painted a dark gray. Gleaming pots and pans hung from a rack in the middle of the room above a large wooden table. A massive espresso machine occupied the better part of the countertop next to the sink —its shiny brass cylinders and pipes looked like some sort of strange science experiment setup.

Camille shook her head. "No," she said.

She turned off the light and then turned to start up the stairs.

Art felt uncomfortable continuing. The professor was not here, and he would likely not be back until they had already left to return home to the States. He may have been Camille's father, but what right did they have rummaging about randomly in his house? Art knew exactly how *his* father would feel about this, and Camille's mother would be furious if she knew where they were and what they were doing. Camille's father may have been a terrible person for what he did to Camille and her mother, but did that give them an excuse to invade his privacy?

Art started to open his mouth to object, when it hit him.

Camille was *not* randomly walking through her father's house.

She was *looking* for something.

The wooden stairs creaked with each step she took.

It must be on the second floor, she thought.

She couldn't get the image out of her mind. It was ridiculous, and Camille knew it. But she had to see it. She had to know it was real. She had seen it so many times over the past month. And if she couldn't see her father, she wanted to see *it.*

She made it to the landing on the second floor. A hallway—identical to the one on the first floor—ran from the stairway back to the front of the house. Immediately past the landing at the top of the stairs was a door. Camille opened it and glanced inside. The room was dark, but she could see what appeared to be a bed situated against the far wall. She closed the door. This was not it.

She made her way toward the front of the house — toward the only other room on the second floor. A set of tall double doors greeted her.

Camille was in her own world.

Art wasn't even sure that she was aware he was standing directly behind her.

She had paused as soon as she had reached the double doors. Light streamed into the second-floor hallway from the window on the front of the townhouse. For a moment everything was still and silent. The only movement was the specks of dust that danced and floated through the rays of light from the afternoon sun.

And then Camille reached out toward the doors and placed her hands on the doorknobs. She turned the knobs and pushed. Stepping inside, Camille disappeared from view.

There was a slight pause.

"I found it," Camille finally said from within the room.

CHAPTER 10

2:22 p.m.
Wednesday, August 13
London, England

Art walked through the doorway.

An assortment of mismatched bookcases lined the walls of the room, all filled to the brim with ancient leather-bound volumes, thick textbooks, and paperbacks. A massive rug covered the floor—a well-worn Persian of faded reds, greens, and blues. Two armchairs sat on the rug—one leather and one cloth, both surrounded by stacks of books. A large birdcage stood near a window on the right side of the room. A parrot with a yellow head and bright green plumage stared at him from his perch.

Sherlock.

"Olfacies sicut simia!" the parrot squawked.

Art didn't speak Latin, but Cos Masters was right—it sure sounded like an insult.

The parrot continued to hurl Latin phrases at him as he made his way into the room. Art started to say something back but caught himself. He didn't need to get into an argument with a parrot, particularly one that spoke Latin.

He turned his attention to the left side of the room. At the far end was a massive wooden desk. It was at least eight feet wide and covered with stacks of papers, even more books, and several coffee cups. But it was the wall behind the desk that really caught Art's attention. It consisted of three sets of shelves that covered the entire width of the wall. The shelves ran from the floor to the ceiling, and each set of shelves was protected by beveled glass doors framed in thick oak with tarnished brass hardware. The shelves were crammed with objects that — in any other context — Art would have expected to find only in a museum. There were several shelves filled with fossils. And these were not the small fish fossils or trilobites that can be bought for a few dollars at some rock and mineral store. There was a large jawbone with thick teeth set in a sand-colored stone matrix, and a small cluster of fossilized eggs — items that could have just as easily been on display at any natural history museum. Other shelves displayed Greek and Roman antiquities, two large marble busts, several collections of coins, and at least twenty clocks and pocket watches. Once more, Art was impressed by Camille's father. And once more, Art reminded himself what Professor Tinsley had done to his friend and her mother.

Art made his way across the room and stood beside Camille in front of the desk. It remained unclear what she had been looking for.

Art expected her to be upset — maybe angry, maybe

crying. To his surprise, there was the slightest hint of a smile on her face.

"I found it," she said again, softly. "It's real."

Art did not immediately say anything. He quickly scanned the desk and the wall for something — anything — that might have been the subject of her search.

But it was useless — the shelves were filled with dozens of items.

"What's real?" Art finally asked. "What were you looking for?"

"That," she said, and nodded. Her eyes continued to scan the desk and wall. She seemed entranced.

"*That*"?

"*That*" *what*?

Art had tried his best to be sensitive to what Camille was going through, but he was wasting time. He needed to be more blunt.

"What are you talking about?" Art asked, a bit louder that he had perhaps intended.

But it worked.

Camille turned to him, the spell apparently broken. "All of it," she said. "He was always sitting at this desk when we Skyped. He told me that this room was his favorite place in the whole world. He told me about all the stuff on the shelves — about all his travels."

Camille paused.

"I just wanted to see this room," she finally said. "I

wanted to see his desk. I wanted to see all of this. I wanted to know it was real."

Camille paused.

"I know that sounds so stupid," she finally said.

"It's not stupid," Art replied. It made complete sense to him. His mother had died when he was four years old, and he had only the vaguest memories of her. But he had a picture of her in which she is holding him and a small stuffed toy — a little pink pig that Art had named Oink. Art still had the stuffed pig, and sometimes alone in his room he would hold it just because of the connection with his mom. It made her real, not just a memory.

CHAPTER 11

Camille ran her hands across the surface of her father's desk. He had told her that it was more than a hundred and fifty years old and that he had purchased it from one of London's oldest accounting firms. It was made of oak, worn and aged to a rich golden color. The desk itself was a mess — piled high with papers, magazines, books, several pens, a stack of letters, and at least five coffee cups.

She glanced up at the wall behind the desk. She knew the stories about how her father had collected each item. She pointed at a sword in a rusted sheath that was in the center set of shelves.

"My dad said that's a nineteenth-century calvary sword," she told Art. "He bought it from some sort of duke of something."

She pointed to a brass padlock with three keys hanging from a hook inside a bell jar. The face of the padlock was intricately engraved with a picture of a tiger. "He bought that in India," she said. "It's some sort of puzzle."

47

She then pointed to a wooden puppet—it was a figure of a bearded man dressed in a long robe and wearing a crown. The puppet's hinged wooden arms hung down from its sides and over the edge of the shelf. It had large eyes and a wide grinning mouth.

"He bought that on a trip to Tibet," she said. "He told me it was haunted."

She started to point to another item when she suddenly paused.

That's strange, she thought.

Something was different about the puppet. She closed her eyes and pictured the brightly colored wooden object in her mind. Her memory of the artifact was particularly vivid. It was one of the creepiest things she had seen in her life, which meant, of course, that she absolutely adored it. Every time she spoke with her father, the puppet would just sit there on the shelf, staring at her through the screen and leaning against the inside of the shelf as if it were simply resting and waiting for the moment to pop up and walk across the room.

That's it.

Camille opened her eyes. The scene in front of her did not match her memory. The puppet was no longer leaning against the inside of the shelf. Instead, it appeared to have been moved closer to the edge of the shelf, and it now seemed to be sitting completely upright.

"What's the matter?" Art asked.

Camille pointed at the puppet.

"He moved," Camille replied.

She's lost it, Art thought.

Camille had not slept in more than twenty-four hours, and it was clear that the strain of the situation with her father had finally gotten to her.

"It didn't move," Art said as delicately as possible. "It's just a puppet. You're probably tired."

Camille shook her head. "Not like that," she said, the exasperation clear in her voice. "I mean it's in a different position. I Skyped with my dad the night before we left, and I'm telling you, it's been moved."

Big deal, Art thought. Maybe Camille was right. Maybe her father had—for some reason—moved the puppet. More likely she was exhausted. Besides, why did it matter?

But apparently it did matter to Camille.

She was already making her way around the desk to get a closer look at the puppet.

CHAPTER 12

2:26 p.m.
Wednesday, August 13
London, England

It had taken a couple weeks before Camille had agreed to Skype with her father. Her mother had done her best to be supportive, but Camille also knew how much her mother distrusted her father. She had urged Camille to take it slow —to keep her father at arm's length.

"Don't get too close to him," her mother had warned.

And although Camille would never do anything to hurt her mother, she couldn't resist the opportunity to see her father face-to-face—even if it was only by Skype. The first call had been awkward. He had asked about school and her friends but not much more. It was clear that he had not spent much time around kids her age. She had asked about an object on the wall behind him—the sword—and he had told her all about it. The call had lasted fewer than ten minutes. But despite how awkward it felt, she couldn't wait for the next call.

He always called her from his office—the very same office in which they were now standing. The conversation always seemed to turn to some item on the shelves. Camille suspected that was on purpose. It gave them something to talk about that didn't involve the hard questions she wanted to ask and the hard answers he wanted to avoid.

She had stared at the shelves behind her father's desk every week for the past month. She knew the puppet had been moved—and that it had been moved within the past day.

Camille was determined to know why.

She stood in front of the center shelf behind her father's desk, the puppet staring back at her from behind the thick glass. Because it had been pushed forward on the shelf, no longer leaning, its upright position now seemed awkward.

But there was more.

The puppet had not simply moved. There was something *behind* the puppet, hidden in the shadowy recesses of the shelf. Camille had never met her father in person, but she knew that the items on the shelves were his prize possessions. They were a reflection of his work, his travels, and his interests. He displayed them so that they could be seen and enjoyed. But whatever was behind the puppet was there for another reason. It was hidden from view—intentionally, it seemed.

"There's something back there," Camille said.

"I don't think we should do this," Art said. "Cos will be back soon."

But Camille was already reaching for the handle to open the glass door on the front of the shelf.

Nothing about this felt right.

What if Cos Masters walked through the door and found Camille rummaging through her father's personal possessions? She would almost certainly tell Camille's father what they had done. She might even contact Camille's mother. Art could only imagine the lectures that would ensue from both Ms. Sullivan and his father about respecting another person's private property. They would probably get grounded—again.

The hinges on the glass door creaked as Camille opened it wide. Art watched as Camille reached inside the shelf. He could hear her shuffling items around.

A hard pit had developed in his stomach.

How would he possibly explain this to Cos Masters? To Ms. Sullivan? To his father?

"Camille said the puppet moved"?

What type of explanation was that?

Art started to open his mouth to object once more, but Camille spoke first.

"That's strange," she said. "Why would he hide this behind the puppet?"

Camille turned around. In her hand she held an hourglass. Less than a foot tall and perhaps four inches wide, it was made of wood and colorfully painted—bright red, gold, and blue. Four thick wooden spindles—attached to chunky bases—held the large glass globes in place. The glass had been etched with a delicate lacelike pattern, and bright white sand filled the lower globe.

In an instant Art forgot all about any explanations that he would have to offer.

They now had a bigger problem.

A much bigger problem.

CHAPTER 13

2:28 p.m.
Wednesday, August 13
London, England

"What's the matter?" Camille asked. The expression on Art's face was one of complete surprise.

"I think I know why your dad suddenly disappeared," he replied.

She glanced down at the hourglass—a simple but ingenious device used for centuries to chart the passage of time. Carefully measured and engineered, it would take precisely an hour for the sand to flow from one globe to the next.

"Because of this?" Camille asked. "It's just an old hourglass."

Art nodded. "It *is* an old hourglass," he agreed. "In fact, it's more than four hundred years old. And it once belonged to a man named John Dee. He was an advisor to Queen Elizabeth I. He was also an astrologer, but some people think he was actually a wizard."

Uh-oh, Camille thought. She had a feeling that this conversation was not heading in a good direction.

"How do you know all of that?" she asked.

"Because," Art replied, "it was stolen two years ago from an exhibit at the Yale Center for British Art."

Art was smart, Camille thought, but how could he be so sure that this was the same hourglass that had been stolen?

There must be a million old hourglasses in the world.

And all hourglasses pretty much look the same, don't they?

Art seemed to anticipate Camille's questions.

"The Yale Center is an art museum," he said.

"Okay, so it's an art museum." Camille replied. "Why does that matter? You might be wrong—this might not be the stolen hourglass."

Art sighed.

"Think about it," he said. "The Yale museum was hosting a major exhibit with paintings, sculptures, and objects worth millions of dollars."

"So?" Camille replied.

"Well," Art continued, "if the museum wanted to hire someone who knew all about preserving old artwork, who would they call?"

Oh.

Camille dreaded saying the answer out loud.

"I would call your dad," Camille finally replied. As a well-respected art conservation scientist, Art's dad had consulted on museum exhibits across the planet.

Art nodded. "And that's exactly what Yale University did. So he was one of the first to find out when the hourglass had gone missing."

"Can I hold it?" Art asked.

Camille—realizing the importance of the ancient and fragile object she held in her hands—was more than happy to hand it over to Art.

"Look here, on the top of the hourglass," Art said. "There are four words."

He turned the hourglass so that she could see the top. A fine dark sand clung to the surface. Art brushed it off, and—just as he had said—there were four words painted on the top: NON HABERI SED ESSE.

"*Non haberi sed esse*," Art said. "It's Latin."

"*Non haberi sed esse!*" Sherlock squawked.

"What does it mean?" Camille asked.

"*Non haberi sed esse!*" Sherlock squawked again.

"I don't speak Latin," Art said, "but I think my dad told me it means 'to be there, but not there'—or something like that."

To be there, but not there?

It was clear that Art was right—Camille's father had hidden a stolen hourglass in his study. And he had done so right before disappearing on a sudden and unexpected trip out of town. It didn't take a rocket scientist to conclude that the two events were probably related.

CHAPTER 14

2:30 p.m.
Wednesday, August 13
London, England

"What now?" Camille asked, returning once more to the question she had asked so often over the course of their adventures. But this time she knew what Art's answer would be. He would point out that the hourglass was stolen and that the right thing to do was to turn it in to the police. Camille also knew the consequences of doing that. The police would almost certainly identify her father as a primary suspect in the theft. And the fact that he had suddenly disappeared would not help him.

She wished that she could rewind the entire afternoon. She had dragged Art out of their hotel rooms to go see a bunch of old stuff on a shelf. It now seemed so silly. And to top it all off, she had managed to find a stolen hourglass hidden in her father's study.

"I think your father may be in trouble," Art said.

Dub.

"I know he's in trouble," Camille replied. "I mean, c'mon, he's hiding a stolen hourglass in his house."

"No," Art replied. "I think . . ."

Art paused, then stared down at the wooden and glass object in his hands.

"Strange . . ." he said, and then paused once more.

Art cradled the hourglass in his left arm and leaned over Professor Tinsley's desk. He looked from one end of the desk to the other, his face just a few inches from the surface. He suddenly stopped and ran his finger across the one clear space on the desk. He raised his finger and showed it to Camille. It was covered in the same dark sand that had been on the top of the hourglass.

"What is it?" Camille asked. She had seen this look in Art's eyes before—she knew it would be difficult getting any answers until her friend had worked through everything in his head.

Art made his way around the desk and squatted down. He ran his finger across the floor and held it up. Several grains of the same dark sand clung to his finger. Art stood back up and held the hourglass out in front of him. He then rotated it over and let the white sand begin to flow from top to bottom. Camille could hear the soft whisper of the sand as it shifted between the globes. Art ran his fingers along the wood base. He held the hourglass to his ear. He gently shook the ancient device.

"Maybe . . ." Art said, his words once more trailing off into silence.

"Maybe what?" Camille asked.

Art did not respond. Instead, he reached over and turned on a lamp on her father's desk. He held the hourglass up next to the light and stared into one globe and then the other.

"There you are!" he exclaimed suddenly.

"What are you talking about?" Camille asked.

Yet again, Art did not respond. Instead, he held one end of the hourglass out toward Camille.

"Hold it tight," he said.

Camille grabbed the end of the hourglass. Before she could ask what he was planning to do, Art had seized the opposite end of the hourglass with both hands. He gave the end a slight counterclockwise twist. Camille could hear the creak of the wood spindles, and she worried that the ancient glass globes would suddenly shatter and spill their sandy contents all over the floor.

"I thought you said this thing was ancient!" Camille exclaimed. "Are you trying to break it?"

Art did not answer. Instead, he gave it a slight clockwise twist. This time the bottom of the hourglass moved ever so slightly.

"Okay, now you've done it," she said. "It's broken. Stolen and broken. That's just great. How are we going to explain this?"

Art ignored her and gave the bottom another clockwise twist. There was a faint click.

A slight grin crossed Art's face. He took the hourglass

from Camille and held it up for her to see. To her surprise, the white sand in the bottom globe started to disappear.

"What'd you do?" asked Camille.

"The base," said Art. "It's hollow. Twisting the bottom opens it up."

"But how did you know?"

"I wasn't sure," he said. "But the hourglass felt lighter than I expected. If the bottom and top bases were made of solid wood, it would've been a lot heavier."

The last of the white sand emptied from the globe into the bottom of the hourglass. They could now see eight circular openings in the base. Art twisted the bottom once again—counterclockwise—and the openings disappeared with a click and a creak. It was as if they never existed.

"But why would it do that?" asked Camille.

"It's just a guess . . ." said Art. He placed his hands on the top of the hourglass and twisted it clockwise until it clicked. He held the hourglass up so they could see inside of it. As with the bottom of the hourglass, eight circles had appeared. But nothing came out.

"It's empty," said Camille.

"Exactly," replied Art.

"Wait," said Camille. "I'm confused. What was in . . ."

She paused for a moment. "The black sand!" she exclaimed. "That's what was in the other end, wasn't it?"

Art smiled and nodded. "I think so," he said. "You can view this hourglass with white sand *or* with black sand. But you have to lock away one color before you use the other —otherwise they will just blend together."

"But how did he get the black sand out? And why?" Camille asked.

"I think I know how," said Art.

He slowly twisted the top of the hourglass in a clockwise direction until it clicked.

"Keep your fingers crossed," he said. Art lifted up on the base but it didn't move. He wiggled it ever so slightly, and the top of the hourglass slowly lifted off, revealing a hollow chamber directly above the glass globe. Small particles of fine black sand still clung to the sides of the chamber.

"Your dad emptied the black sand for a reason," said Art. "He left the white sand, but he didn't want anyone to fill the globes with black sand."

"But why not?" asked Camille.

"I think I know," he said. "Cos Masters will be back any minute, and we need to fill it back up with black sand to see if I'm right."

"How?" Camille asked. "There isn't enough black sand on the desk or the floor to fill a spoon."

"Maybe your father dumped it in the trash can," suggested Art, "or hid it somewhere."

They checked the trash can, but it was empty. They checked the drawers in the desk, the coffee cups, and a pencil holder.

There was no sign of the sand—just the small remains on the desk and floor.

It was clear that whatever Camille's father had done with the dark sand, he had not left it in his office for anyone to find.

They were running out of time.

Art looked around the room in desperation for something to replace the black sand, but there was nothing.

CHAPTER 15

2:32 p.m.
Wednesday, August 13
London, England

"I have an idea," Art said.

Before Camille could respond, he had sprinted from the room. Now it was Camille's time to worry — Cos Masters would be back any minute, and Camille was standing by her father's desk with a stolen ancient hourglass.

Camille made her way over to the window at the front of the house and glanced up the narrow lane. There was no sign of Cos Masters — yet.

What is Art doing?

Art threw open one cabinet after another.

It had to be here.

It was the only thing that would work.

He knew that at any moment Cos Masters would walk back through the front door.

There was no time to waste. He had to find it.

Camille glanced back out the window.

There was still no sign of Cos Masters.

Her heart was beating a mile a minute. She just wanted to put the hourglass back behind the puppet, forget that they had ever found it, and go back to their hotel.

He had looked in every cabinet.

He had checked the drawers.

He had checked the pantry.

He had even checked the small tin containers on the kitchen table.

It was nowhere to be found, and he was rapidly running out of time.

The only place he hadn't checked was . . .

Of course, he realized. *The freezer!*

She couldn't take it anymore.

They just needed to return the hourglass to where they had found it. Camille made her way quickly back across the room and grabbed the hourglass off the desk. She was just about to put the cap back onto the top of the hourglass when she heard them — footsteps.

Her heart skipped a beat.

Has Cos Masters managed to get back in the house?

Maybe there was a back door.

Camille stood there, behind her father's desk, holding the stolen hourglass.

But it wasn't Cos Masters.

It was Art.

He sprinted across the office and set a silver can on the desk.

"Espresso!" he exclaimed. "Ground espresso beans."

Art opened the top of the can and showed the finely ground coffee beans to Camille.

"Nice try," Camille said. "But it won't work."

"Why not?" Art asked.

Camille knew all about espresso. It was the go-to ingredient in almost every drink at Starbucks and every other coffee shop. And her mother loved to drink the dark, bitter coffee. But as clever as Art may have been, he had forgotten one particularly important thing about espresso. She stuck her finger in the can and removed it. Espresso — unlike regular coffee — was basically a powder. The espresso clung to her finger.

"There's no way it will pour like sand from one globe to the next," she said. "And even if it did pour like sand, this is an hourglass — and we don't have an hour. We just need to put the hourglass back where we found it before Cos Masters gets back."

Art smiled and held up a small plastic coffee stirrer. "I thought you might say that," he said.

"What are you going to do with that?" asked Camille.

"Just watch," replied Art. He took the plastic stirrer and plunged it into the can of ground espresso beans. He then removed the stirrer, stuck it into the top globe of the hour-glass, and blew on the end of the stirrer.

POOF.

A cloud of espresso exploded in the globe and coated the interior with the dark powdery substance.

"Okay," Camille said, "I didn't see that coming."

Art set the straw aside and examined the globe.

He wasn't sure what he had expected to happen, but there was nothing there—just a globe coated with dark espresso powder.

"Maybe the black sand had something to do with the bottom globe," suggested Camille.

Art quickly refilled the stirrer with ground espresso and pushed the straw down through the hourglass to where the top and bottom globe met.

He took a deep breath and blew again.

POOF.

The cloud of dark espresso powder covered the interior of the bottom globe.

Camille gasped.

As if by magic, words had appeared on the bottom globe—a fine white script revealed by the dark espresso:

> *In weak field whence youth depart'd,*
> *three made one ye sign impart'd.*
> *Whence youth now sleeps three saints reside,*
> *ye second signs held by her side.*
> *O'er ye heavens youth was crowned,*
> *ye signs reveal what time hath bound.*

"There but not there," said Art. *"Non haberi sed esse."*

"Wow," said Camille. "The words were hidden in all of the white stuff carved on the glass, and you couldn't see any of it with the white sand."

They both stood and stared at the words that had appeared.

And that's when they heard it.

The front door.

Camille looked at Art.

Cos Masters had returned.

CHAPTER 16

2:35 p.m.
Wednesday, August 13
London, England

"Camille! Art!" Cos Masters called out. "Are you still here?"

"Uh, yes," Camille replied. "We're upstairs . . . Uh . . . be down in a minute."

Camille cringed. Could that have sounded any more suspicious?

They could hear footsteps in the hallway below them. "I'll be right up," Cos replied. "I have to feed Sherlock."

Camille took out her phone and quickly snapped a couple of pictures of the bottom globe with her cell. They would have to figure out what the poem meant later.

"Art," said Camille. "We have to . . ."

But Art was already one step ahead of her.

He grabbed the cap of the hourglass and snapped it back into place. Then he twisted the bottom base so that the eight holes were showing. He turned the hourglass over and the white sand immediately started pouring down into the top globe, covering the espresso powder and the poem.

The footsteps were now ascending the stairs.

Camille grabbed the hourglass and slid it back into place behind the puppet. Art carefully closed the glass door on the front of the shelves. It produced a slight creak and a click, which caused both Art and Camille to wince.

The footsteps were now in the hallway.

Art turned back around and did his best to sweep the remaining black sand from the desk. They couldn't take any chances that someone else might find out what was happening.

They had just managed to return to the far side of the desk when Cos Masters entered the room carrying a bag of bird feed.

"*Non haberi sed esse!*" Sherlock called out as she entered. "*Non haberi sed esse!*"

Cos Masters shook her head. "That bird," she said. "I swear I'm going to learn Latin just so I know what he's saying about me."

Art, Camille, and Cos Masters stood on the sidewalk outside Professor Tinsley's home. Sherlock had been fed, and the house had been locked.

"It was a pleasure meeting you," Cos said as she extended her hand to both of them. "Unfortunately, I have to be going. I have a class to teach this afternoon."

"Do you mind if I ask a question before you go?" Camille said.

"Not at all," replied Cos Masters.

"Has my father ever done this before?" Camille asked. "You know, just disappeared without any warning."

Cos Masters shuffled her feet. The question clearly made her uncomfortable. "Your father is a great many things," she said. "He is brilliant and frustrating in equal measure. But I have never known him to be impulsive. I texted him back last night and asked what was going on, but he didn't respond. Quite frankly, I'm worried about him."

And for good reason, Art thought. It was clear that Professor Tinsley had not called upon Cos Masters for any help other than to take care of Sherlock. There was no delicate way to ask the next question, so he just needed to ask it.

"If Professor Tinsley was . . . in trouble," Art asked, "is there someone he might go to?"

Cos Masters did not immediately respond.

"Sixty-five Cecil Court," she finally said. "Ask for Eunice."

"Who's Eunice?" Art asked.

"The only person who might know what is going on," Cos Masters responded.

Cos Masters walked with Camille and Art to the square, where they went their separate ways. Cos Masters glanced over her shoulder as the boy and the girl turned the corner and disappeared.

She worried that she had made a mistake—that she had overstepped.

But if Art and Camille were looking for answers, they might be found at 65 Cecil Court.

However, they might not be the answers the two were seeking.

CHAPTER 17

Art and Camille exited the Charing Cross Underground Station, walked across Trafalgar Square, and stood on the front steps of the National Gallery. The view was magnificent. In the distance—at the far end of Parliament Street—stood Elizabeth Tower, more commonly known by the name of its massive iron bell, Big Ben. Behind Art and Camille was the broad stone edifice of the National Gallery, one of the world's most important and most visited art museums. Art's father had frequently consulted with the museum, and Art had spent hours upon hours roaming its labyrinth of galleries.

"There." Camille pointed. "We can tell my mom we stopped by the National Gallery."

She briefly consulted the map on her phone and then headed back down the steps. Art followed. He was worried about Camille. She had been on an emotional roller coaster since arriving in London that morning.

"Maybe we should have told your mother what we

73

found," Art said, a suggestion he had made several times since leaving Professor Tinsley's home.

"I'm pretty sure I know how she would feel about this," Camille replied.

Camille was right.

"Your mom's pretty mad about your father," Art said.

Camille nodded. "Mom thinks he ran away again," she said, "just like he did before I was born. Did you know that's why my mom became a foster parent? She wanted kids to have someone who cared about them when no one else would."

"He did run away again," Art said. "Just not for the reasons your mom thinks."

Art hesitated for a moment. "But . . . what if he isn't who you think he is?" he finally asked. "You know . . . the whole hourglass thing. Whatever is going on, your father's definitely in the middle of it."

Camille didn't respond.

Camille and Art made their way north along Charing Cross Road. Neither spoke.

After a five-minute walk, they reached the entrance to Cecil Court, a narrow passageway that connected Charing Cross Road to St Martin's Lane. The thoroughfare was filled with bookstores and antique dealers. Hand-lettered signs of every size and shape hung from poles attached to painted cast-iron façades. Sandwich boards—large folding signs that shopkeepers would place outside each morning—stood at attention in front of several stores, enticing those passing by to stop in and browse.

Camille came to a halt and turned to Art.

"He's not a thief," she said. "I just know. I don't know how I know, I just do."

3:25 p.m.
Wednesday, August 13
65 Cecil Court
London, England

Art and Camille looked up at the dark green sign with faded yellow letters hanging over the entrance to the store. It read

WALLACE & MEATH

PROPRIETORS OF FINE BOOKS, MANUSCRIPTS, AND MAPS

SINCE 1853

65 CECIL COURT

"This is it," Camille said as she opened the door and stepped inside. A tarnished silver bell attached to the top of the door signaled their arrival. Art followed close behind and pulled the door shut. Small and narrow with a low ceiling crossed by exposed wooden beams, the bookstore smelled of dust and black tea. To their left was a tall wooden counter with an ancient brass cash register. Wooden shelves filled with books crowded the shop. A sign at the back of the store pointed to a set of narrow wooden stairs and reminded customers that maps and manuscripts could be found on the floor above.

"Is anyone here?" whispered Camille.

"It's not a library," replied Art. "There's no need to whisper."

Art went over to one of the bookcases. He ran his finger along the spines of several leather-bound books. "They're all about European history," he said. "England, Spain, France, Denmark . . . They just go on and on."

He scooted over to the next bookshelf, then the next and then the next. It was all the same.

"Is that why Cos sent us here?" Camille asked. Her father *was* a professor of history. Did his disappearance have something to do with that? Maybe he was researching something about the hourglass.

Their discussion was interrupted by the sound of footsteps in the room directly above their heads.

"I'll be right down," a woman's voice called from above. "Please feel free to browse around a bit."

Camille and Art listened as the footsteps made their

way over and then down the stairs at the rear of the store. An exceedingly tall, gray-haired woman emerged from the stairwell. She stared at Camille and Art over a pair of half-moon reading glasses attached to a long chain around her neck.

"Oh," she said. "Children."

Camille bristled at the woman's condescending tone. She noticed from the corner of her eye that Art had immediately straightened up to his full height.

"Are your parents about?" asked the woman as she made her way over to the entrance and placed her hand on the doorknob.

"No, ma'am," replied Camille.

"Then perhaps you should find them," the woman suggested as she opened the door.

"Actually," said Camille, "we came here to see someone named Eunice."

The woman pulled the door shut. "I am Eunice," she said. "What business do you have with me?"

The condescending tone in her voice remained, but Camille was not deterred.

"My name is Camille Sullivan," she said, "and this is my friend Art. We are looking for my father. His name is Broderick Tinsley. He's a professor at University College, and he disappeared this morning. We were told that you might be able to help us?"

"And who told you that?" the woman asked.

"Cos Masters," Camille replied. "She's a professor at the college."

"I am afraid that Professor Masters is incorrect," the gray-haired woman replied.

This was looking more and more like a dead end.

"Show her the riddle," Art suggested.

The woman peered down over her glasses at Camille. "What riddle?"

Camille took out her phone and pulled up a photo of the poem on the hourglass.

"I think his disappearance has something to do with this," said Camille.

The woman examined the photo and then handed the phone back to Camille. "I'm quite certain that I have no idea what this is all about."

Camille and Art stared at each other. The woman standing in front of them did not seem the least bit inclined to help. Cos Masters had been wrong.

The gray-haired woman pushed the front door open once again. "I'm sorry I could not be of assistance," she said.

Camille did not think the woman sounded sorry.

Art put his hand on Camille's arm. "Let's go."

Camille nodded. She followed Art through the front door and then turned and faced the woman. "If you think of anything," Camille said, "we're staying at the Barbican Thistle Hotel."

The woman did not respond.

Camille closed the door behind her and departed.

Eunice watched as the young girl and her friend made their way back toward Charing Cross Road. She waited until they had melted into the crowd, and then she locked the entrance to the store and placed a sign in the window indicating she would reopen the following morning.

She had not been honest with the girl about a number of things.

She knew more about the riddle than she had let on.

CHAPTER 18

4:15 p.m.
Wednesday, August 13
London, England

At first blush, the map of the London Underground—the city's famous subway system known locally as the Tube— appeared hopelessly confusing. A variety of colored lines —green, yellow, red, brown, and more—crisscrossed in every direction. The map bore only a faint relationship to the actual layout of the ancient city. In reality, however, the Tube was remarkably easy to use—thanks in large part to the map itself. Getting from one station to the next was simple—all a tourist had to know were a direction and a color. North on the yellow line to Notting Hill Gate. South on the brown line to Oxford Circus. Londoners, of course, forwent the colors and referred to the lines by their given names. North on Circle line to Notting Hill Gate. South on Bakerloo to Oxford Circus. The colors, names, and directions were clearly identified in each underground station. A newcomer to London could comfortably make his or her way from South Ruislip to Upminster Bridge—a trip that covered the entire width of London and beyond—with relative ease.

Art and Camille took Bakerloo south from Charing Cross to Embankment and then caught the Circle line east on the way to Barbican, the station closest to their hotel.

They were fortunate enough to secure a couple of seats on the busy train and settled in for the ride.

"Can I see the riddle?" Art asked again.

Camille pulled up a picture on her phone and handed it to Art.

In weak field whence youth depart'd,
three made one ye sign impart'd.
Whence youth now sleeps three saints reside,
ye second signs held by her side.
O'er ye heavens youth was crowned,
ye signs reveal what time hath bound.

Art was frustrated. He had no idea where to even start in solving the riddle. He had already Googled most of the terms in the poem, individually and in a variety of combinations, all to no avail. He had no answers to give. Part of the problem was that the riddle had been written more than four hundred years ago. The meaning of words changes over time. Landmarks disappear. People are forgotten. And what if it wasn't even a riddle? Maybe it was just a silly poem, nothing more.

"Maybe your father would help us with the riddle?" Camille suggested.

"I thought about that," Art replied. "But I know what he would do. He was one of the first people they had called when the hourglass was stolen. This would be personal for him. He would report this to the police immediately, and I just can't put him in that position."

Art paused.

"It looks like we're on our own," he finally said.

5:30 p.m.
Wednesday, August 13
The Berkeley Hotel
London, England

Broderick stood on the balcony outside his hotel room, sipped a cup of tea, and listened to the sounds of the city below. It would be a wonderful place to stay if he were on vacation.

But he was not on vacation.

He stepped back into his suite, closed the patio door, and went into the bedroom. Neatly arranged on the bed were five black cases. Each case was constructed of a high-impact plastic polymer and fitted with precision-cut foam inserts. Stainless-steel hardware held the cases tightly and securely closed.

Broderick had questioned whether all of this was really necessary. It would be very simple, he had explained to

Davenport. They could be in and out in less than an hour.

"But what if it's not simple?" Miles Davenport had asked. "What if you're wrong?"

Davenport was right, of course. There was too much at stake. And they would not get a second chance. He needed to be prepared.

Broderick opened the nearest case. Inside was a small metal box with a curved black handle. The device was no bigger than a shoebox. A control pad with a video screen, a set of cables, and a thick instruction manual was also included. This particular device, Davenport had explained, cost around fifty thousand dollars.

"Be careful with it," he had warned him.

Broderick pulled out the manual, settled into a large chair in the corner of the room, and started reading.

CHAPTER 19

7:41 p.m.
Wednesday, August 13
London, England

Dinner had been difficult.

Camille's mom had returned from her meetings shortly after five o'clock and herded Camille and Art out the door to a local restaurant. Camille knew the situation with her father had not been easy for her mom, and Camille also knew how much her mother would be hurt if she found out how Camille and Art had spent the afternoon. Camille tried to keep the conversation at dinner on anything but her father. They had not exactly lied to her mother about what they had done; they had just not provided the precise details.

We walked around the city.

We stopped by the National Gallery.

We rode the Tube.

But as much as Camille tried to convince herself that she was not lying to her mom, she knew that the details mattered.

They returned to the hotel after dinner and settled

into their rooms. The problem, however, was that they were no closer to finding out what the riddle meant than when they had first discovered it. Art, because he had a room to himself, was free to continue to search the Internet for any clues as to the riddle's meaning. But his efforts — as before — failed to bring any further clarity.

Camille's mother had another full schedule of business meetings the following day, which would provide the perfect opportunity for Art and Camille to continue their efforts to uncover what had happened to her father. But the one clue that they had in their possession had proved so far to be utterly useless.

Mary Sullivan had decided to take a long hot shower, and Camille had just changed into her pajamas and settled into bed to watch television when there was a knock on the door.

Camille made her way over and glanced through the peephole. A young woman dressed in a hotel uniform stood outside. Camille cracked open the door.

"Is something wrong?" Camille asked.

The young woman smiled and shook her head. "No, ma'am," she replied. "Are you Camille Sullivan?"

"Yes," Camille replied.

The young woman handed Camille a small envelope. "Someone dropped off a message for you," she said.

A message for me?

"Who?" Camille asked.

"I don't know," the young woman replied. "It was left at the front desk. I was just asked to deliver it to your room."

Camille glanced over at the door to the bathroom. She could still hear the shower running, and her mother had just started singing some song from the 1980s.

"Thank you," Camille said as she closed the door.

Camille opened the small envelope. Inside was a small note card with a handwritten inscription. It read:

NPG 2457

Tomorrow

10:00 a.m.

Camille turned the card over, but there was no indication as to who had sent it. She retrieved her phone from the bedside table and took a photo of the card. Whatever the card meant, Camille sensed that it was not something she wanted her mother to know about—at least not yet. She folded up the card and envelope and placed them in her luggage.

She pulled up the photo on her phone and texted it to Art.

Camille sighed.

She was getting tired of riddles.

* * *

Art had brushed his teeth and settled into bed to watch a rugby match when he received the text from Camille.

Any clue what this means? she wrote. *It sounds like we are supposed to be somewhere tomorrow, but where?*

Art smiled. The riddle on the hourglass may have stumped him, but he knew exactly what the note on the card meant.

CHAPTER 20

8:32 a.m.
Thursday, August 14
London, England

NPG—Art explained the next morning over breakfast—stood for National Portrait Gallery.

A confused look immediately appeared on Camille's face.

"The museum where your father works?" Camille asked. "In Washington, DC?"

"No," Art replied. "The one in London."

Art explained that the gallery in London was actually the oldest museum in the world dedicated to displaying portraits, predating the National Portrait Gallery in Washington, DC, by more than a hundred years.

"Still," Camille noted, "you have to admit that's very confusing. I think one of them should change their name. Maybe the London Portrait Gallery, or the United States Portrait Gallery. Or maybe the Gallery of United States Portraits, and they could call it the GUSP. That's pretty good—the GUSP."

"I'll suggest that to my dad right away," Art replied.

"So what about the number—2457?" she asked.

"Every painting in the museum has a number," Art explained. "I think we are supposed to meet whoever sent the note in the gallery where painting 2457 is located."

"So whose portrait is painting 2457?" Camille asked.

Art told her.

"Wait, what?" Camille replied. "I don't even know who that is. What does he have to do with any of this?"

Art shrugged. He had been asking himself that same question since the previous night.

CHAPTER 21

They stood in front of portrait number 2457.

It was a painting of a man—an ancient portrait painted around the year 1540 A.D. by an unknown artist.

The background was blood red. In the painting the man gazed to his right, his hands clasped in front of him. He wore a black shirt trimmed in gold and white. Wisps of auburn hair curled out from beneath a black cap.

"King Henry VI," Art said.

Camille had heard of King Henry VIII, but not King Henry VI. Of course she understood that in order to have a King Henry VIII, there had to be numbers one through seven. But she knew absolutely nothing about Henry VI (or numbers one through five, or number seven, for that matter), and Art could not offer much more about King Henry VI than what he had read on Wikipedia the night before.

"He was, by all accounts, a terrible king," a woman's

voice behind them said. "Mind you, not a terrible person — he just wasn't very good at his job."

Art and Camille turned to find Eunice, the woman from the bookstore, standing behind them.

"You?" Camille exclaimed. "You sent the note?"

The woman nodded. "I must apologize for yesterday," she said, "but your sudden appearance took me by surprise."

Her tone was surprisingly warm, almost friendly. But Camille was having none of it. The woman had been so rude and — even worse — condescending the previous day. Had she called them to the museum simply to apologize?

"Why did you send the note?" Camille asked. Her tone was cool and matter-of-fact. She normally did not speak to adults — or anyone — in this manner, but the reception they had received the previous afternoon still rankled her.

"Because I believe I know what the riddle means," the woman said.

Eunice took a seat on a long couch in the middle of the gallery and motioned for Camille and Art to join her.

They sat facing the portrait of the king.

"King Henry VI?" Art asked. "Does he have something to do with the riddle? Is that why you asked us to meet you here?"

"Actually," explained Eunice, "he has *everything* to do with the riddle."

Eunice asked Camille to pull up the photo of the riddle and read the first part of the first line.

"In weak field whence youth depart'd," Camille said.

"Have you ever heard of an anagram?" Eunice asked.

"Yes," Art replied. "It's where you take all of the letters from one word and jumble them up to form another word."

"Precisely," said Eunice.

"So," Camille interjected, "an anagram for Art would be . . . rat? Rat? Rat Hamilton?"

Art rolled his eyes. "Ignore her," he said.

"Well, you are both correct," said Eunice. "An anagram is a word remixed into another word. The phrase 'weak field' immediately jumped out at me when you showed me the riddle. It didn't make a lot of sense in the context of the riddle —and since it's the first word of any significance, I decided to start there."

"And you found something?" Camille asked.

"I did," Eunice replied. "I suspected from the other clues in the riddle that it had something to do with Henry VI—the anagram absolutely confirmed it."

"That must have taken hours," Art said. He imagined Eunice with a pad of paper, writing down combination after combination.

"Not at all," said Eunice. "I used the Internet. There are all sorts of anagram generators. You simply type in a word or phrase, and the anagram generator will spit out every conceivable word or phrase that includes that particular combination of letters. It took me two minutes, maybe less. I knew the word as soon as I saw it."

It took Art mere seconds to find an anagram generator on his phone and type in the words "weak field." He stared at the results.

"The anagram generator produced only one complete word," Art said. "Lots of partial words and phrases—but only one complete word."

"And that word is . . .?" Eunice asked.

"Wakefield," replied Art.

"And therein lies the answer to your riddle," said Eunice. "Or at least the first part of it."

Art and Camille stared at the older woman. No one spoke.

"All right," Camille finally said. "I have to ask—how exactly does that solve the riddle? Am I missing something?"

Eunice pointed to the painting. "King Henry VI became king when he was only nine months old," she said.

"Whoa," Camille said. "A baby king? How does that even work?"

Camille then paused for a moment.

"Wait," she finally said, "he's the 'youth' in the riddle, isn't he?"

Eunice nodded.

"But what does it mean that he departed?" Camille said. "Where did he go?"

"It's not where he went," Art said. "It's what happened."

Art had been rereading the short bio of the king on Wikipedia as Camille and Eunice spoke.

"And what happened?" asked Eunice. From the tone in her voice, it was clear that she already knew the answer.

"He was murdered," Art replied. "The riddle is saying he 'departed' life."

"And where was he murdered?" Eunice asked, once more leading them toward her intended destination.

"At the Tower of London," Art replied.

"The Tower of London?" Camille said. "The place where the Crown Jewels are kept? Mom wanted us to go on a tour of it. That's cool and all, but I still don't get it—what does that have to do with Wakefield or the riddle?"

"Because," Eunice said, "the Tower of London is actually made up of several different towers: the White Tower, the Bloody Tower, the Bell Tower, the Cradle Tower, and on and on. But do you want to guess the name of the tower where the king was murdered?"

The pieces suddenly fell into place for Camille.

"Wakefield Tower," she replied.

CHAPTER 22

10:10 a.m.
Thursday, August 14
Gallery One, National Portrait Gallery
London, England

Camille stared at the painting of King Henry VI. She had not expected the first part of the riddle to involve the death of a king.

"And what about the second part of that line?" Camille asked. "'Three made one ye sign impart'd'? What does that mean?"

Eunice sighed. "I'm afraid I've carried you as far as I can," she said. "I've tried—I just haven't been able to decipher the second part. But I think you know where to find the answer."

"The Tower of London," said Camille.

"And the next line?" asked Art. "'Whence youth now sleeps.' Sleep means death, right?"

Eunice nodded appreciatively. "Henry VI's tomb—where he sleeps—is in St George's Chapel at Windsor Castle. "

Camille looked up from her phone—she had joined Art in quickly scanning the biography of the king. "'O'er ye heavens youth was crowned.' The third line of the riddle. It says on Wikipedia that Henry VI was crowned at Westminster Abbey."

"Yes," replied Eunice. "The Tower of London, Windsor Castle, and then Westminster Abbey. Quite peculiar, don't you think? You're going to have to go to each location to decipher the rest of the clues."

Camille, Art, and Eunice stood outside the entrance to the National Portrait Gallery.

"Thank you for your help," Camille said. "I don't know what's going on with my dad, but I want to find out."

"We wouldn't even know where to start if it wasn't for you," Art added.

Eunice shrugged. "It's the least I could do," she said, "particularly after the way I treated the two of you yesterday."

"Well, we did sorta surprise you," Camille acknowledged.

A slight smile creased Eunice's face. "That you did," she said.

Eunice reached into her purse and retrieved a small rectangular piece of paper. She handed it to Camille.

"My business card," Eunice said. "Please let me know what you find out about your father."

The older lady bent down and looked Camille directly in the eyes. She placed her hand on Camille's shoulder.

"I wouldn't worry too much about your father," she said. "I've known him for a long time. He's probably neck deep in research at some library or museum and doesn't even realize what day it is. I don't mean to be cruel, but he has a history of rushing off at the most inopportune times."

Camille nodded. "I know," she said.

"I suppose you do," Eunice replied.

"So where do we start?" asked Camille excitedly as soon as Eunice had departed. "The Tower of London? Windsor Castle? Westminster Abbey?"

They had not told Eunice about the stolen hourglass. Perhaps, Art thought, it was time they told someone. A riddle may have been involved, but it was clear to Art that this was not a game.

"Maybe we should tell—" Art started to say.

"No," Camille interrupted. "Not yet."

"But—" Art tried to continue.

Camille interrupted once more. "No."

Then she paused.

"I know we can't keep this a secret forever," she finally said. "But we have one more day before we head home. Can we at least see what we can find out before then?"

Art knew how desperately Camille wanted to get to know her father—to have some sort of relationship with him. Even though her father had hurt her when he hadn't shown up at the airport the previous morning, the mere possibility that she might be able to help him in some small way meant the world to her right now.

"We start with the Tower," Art said. It was probably a dead end, he thought, but at least it would keep them occupied. It was better than sitting alone in a hotel room all day.

"But why the Tower?" Camille asked. "Why not Windsor Castle, or Westminster Abbey?"

"Because," Art said, "whoever wrote the riddle intended for us to start at the Tower. Think about it. The second line ends with 'second signs held by her side.' Second, not first."

Camille nodded. "I guess that makes sense," she said.

"And," Art continued, "the last part of the final line —'ye signs reveal what time hath bound'—clearly means we have to have the 'signs' from the Tower of London and Windsor Castle before we get to Westminster Abbey."

Art paused. "If we make it that far," he finally said. "We've only got one day, and that's a lot to cover."

Camille smiled. "Then I guess today is my lucky day," she said.

Art looked confused. "What do you mean?"

"Because I have Rat Hamilton on my side," she replied.

CHAPTER 23

More than two million visitors a year toured the grounds of the Tower of London. They dutifully listened to the audio guides and carefully followed the prescribed paths around and throughout the imposing structures. They gaped at the Crown Jewels and marveled at the vast collection of ancient armor and weapons in the White Tower. They posed for photographs in front of impressive stone structures and on emerald green lawns. They spent vast sums at the gift shop —memories to be shared with their families back home, wherever home may be. For most of these visitors, the Tower ultimately became little more than a collection of photographs on Facebook and Instagram.

The Tower, however, was so much more.

The Tower was London. The Tower was England.

The Tower consisted of numerous buildings, tall stone walls, narrow walkways and passages, wide green lawns, and gateways built over many centuries. The original Tower structure—the White Tower, as it had been and was still known—dated back almost a thousand years. That same structure had once been protected by Roman walls built a thousand years earlier. The Tower of London had served as a palace, a fortress, and a prison. It had served as a refuge for kings and as the final resting place for traitors. It had survived war, rebellion, plague, and the great fires that had once ravaged London on a regular basis.

The history of the Tower was, quite literally, inscribed in its stones. Over the centuries, prisoners had engraved upon its walls their thoughts, their hopes, their despairs, and their prayers. On April 2, 1559, William Rame—a prisoner in Beauchamp Tower of whom nothing else was known besides his name—carved upon the wall: "Use well the time of prosperity and remember the time of misfortune."

It was an appropriate motto for the Tower itself.

Camille stood at the railing near the entrance to the Tower and looked down at the broad lawn that had once served as a moat. It was a beautiful sunny day, and the grass was a brilliant green. She could see the top floors of the majestic White Tower rising in the middle of the vast Tower complex.

It was all very impressive.

But they were running out of time.

Where was Art with the tickets?

Camille finally caught sight of him hurrying across the

plaza in front of the ticket office. He held up two tickets and a guide map.

"What took you so long?" she asked.

Art pointed toward the long line at the ticket office. "It's the most popular tourist spot in London," Art said. "What did you expect?"

Camille grabbed Art by the arm and pulled him in the direction of the entrance. They showed their tickets at the main gate and then crossed the stone bridge that once spanned the Tower's moat.

They made their way down a stone passageway next to the tall outer walls of the Tower complex. The morning sun had yet to reach the walkway, and the shadows remained deep and cool. The high walls blocked any view of the modern city of London. A Yeoman Warder—more popularly known as a Beefeater—passed them dressed in the ancient guard uniform they had worn for centuries. It was as if they had been transported eight hundred years back in time.

"How do we get to Wakefield Tower?" Camille asked.

Art consulted the guide map and then pointed to a large round tower ahead of them and to their left. Built of stone and rising at least three stories in the air, the tower was connected to the outer wall by an arched walkway. "That's Wakefield Tower," he said. "The guide map says it's part of the tour of the Medieval Palace."

"Palace?" Camille said, glancing around. "What palace? This place looks like a prison."

"The Medieval Palace is built into the walls of the Tower," Art replied. He pointed to a stone stairway to their right. A small sign with an arrow pointing up the stairway read: MEDIEVAL PALACE & SOUTH WALL WALK.

"That's where the tour starts," he said. "Up the stairs, through St Thomas's Tower, over Traitors' Gate, across the elevated walkway, and into Wakefield Tower."

"Traitors' Gate?" said Camille. "Sure sounds like a prison to me."

Art glanced up at the high stone walls. He couldn't disagree with Camille's assessment.

CHAPTER 24

Camille and Art proceeded up the narrow stone staircase leading into the Medieval Palace and a large, unfurnished room. A massive stone fireplace occupied one side of the room. The ancient walls had been stripped bare, exposing the brick, stone, and timber underneath. Art stopped and glanced at the large display in the middle of the room.

"This is the Hall of the Medieval Palace," he said. "It's almost eight hundred years old."

Camille ignored Art, who—given the opportunity—would read every label and sign in a museum. She wasn't here to be a tourist. Camille pushed through the crowd to the next room in St Thomas's Tower—a sign identified it as King Edward I's bedchamber. Art followed close behind.

The bedchamber—in contrast to the room they had just departed—had been restored to appear as it had when the king lived there in the year 1294. The walls were painted a brilliant white with a rose pattern that repeated throughout the room. The king's ornate bed was draped with a bright red canopy that hung from chains extended between tall green bedposts. The fireplace was huge, decorated with colorful tiles and large enough for a man to stand inside. A thick velvet rope kept tourists from entering the restored portion of the room.

Camille spotted the sign pointing in the direction of Wakefield Tower.

"This way," she said.

At the far end of the room they found a guard standing in front of a narrow timber-framed doorway. They could see a stone archway and a set of stone stairs curling off to the left behind the guard.

"Is this the way to Wakefield Tower?" asked Camille.

"Aye," said the guard, a short man with gray hair trimmed tight against his head.

"Is it open?" asked Camille.

The guard pointed to a sign on a tripod behind him. It read:

WAKEFIELD TOWER IS CLOSED FOR THE DAY.

PLEASE RETURN TO THE ENTRANCE TO THE MEDIEVAL PALACE

FOR AN ALTERNATIVE ROUTE TO THE WALL WALK.

WE APOLOGIZE FOR ANY INCONVENIENCE.

"Closed?" asked Camille. "But I have to get in there."

"Sorry, young miss," replied the guard. "But that's orders. Wakefield is closed for the day."

"Why is it closed?" asked Art.

"Filming some sort of documentary," said the guard. "They spent most of the morning lugging film equipment in there."

Camille and Art walked back toward the entrance to King Edward's bedchamber.

"Well," Art said, "I would suggest that we come back tomorrow, but we can't do that, can we?"

"No," said Camille. "We have to get in there now."

"Maybe I can talk the guard into letting us take a peek," Art said. "You know, tell him we are heading home tomorrow and this is our last chance. Maybe he'll feel sorry for us. That might work."

Camille paused and looked around the room. It was packed with people. Closing off access to Wakefield Tower meant that the crowds of tourists had to loop back to exit the room, effectively doubling the number of people who would normally be in the room.

Camille smiled. She had an idea.

"Just leave it to me," she said.

CHAPTER 25

10:48 a.m.
Thursday, August 14
Tower of London
London, England

Camille instructed Art to stand near the entrance to Wakefield Tower but not so close as to attract the guard's attention. So Art made his way back through the crowd until he was just a few feet from where the guard stood. Hanging on the wall to the guard's right was a flat-screen television. A video describing the history of the bedchamber played on the screen. Art stood in front of the flat screen and pretended to watch the video.

Camille walked to the far side of the room and stood at the spot where the velvet rope attached to the wall. The rope separated the crowd of tourists from the restored bedchamber. She looked down. The rope was attached to an iron ring in the wall by means of a simple hook.

Perfect.

Camille glanced to her left. She could no longer see the guard due to the increasing size of the crowd—and the guard could no longer see her. Camille checked to her right. Nothing but tourists.

Ever so casually, she placed her right hand on the hook and then leaned over the rope as if she were trying to get a better look at the bedchamber. With her body blocking any view of the hook and iron ring, she carefully removed the hook from the wall, flipped it over, and hung it upside down on the iron ring. She placed the hook so that the tip barely rested on the iron ring. Any slight movement of the velvet rope would dislodge it instantly from the wall.

Henry Defessus stood and watched the crowd in the bedchamber grow bigger and bigger. Henry had worked as a security guard at the Tower for twelve years following his retirement from the National Rail service. The Tower, he well knew, was always crowded—but never like this.

Stupid is what it is—shutting down Wakefield Tower for the day.

Henry took several deep breaths in an effort to maintain his composure. There was no sense in getting worked up so early in the day.

"I can't see!" screamed Anne Atkinson. The five-year-old stood on her tiptoes in front of her mother and strained to see the exhibits in the bedchamber.

"Just be patient," said her mother. "A spot will open up soon."

Delores Atkinson could not wait for the day to end—and it had only just started. Anne was a precious and smart child—but patience was not her strong suit, and this was only the first stop in their tour of the Tower. They had taken the train into London from their home in Bedford that same morning, and it had been a miserable trip. Anne had complained, argued, and cried for most of the hour-and-ten-minute ride. As soon as they had entered the Tower grounds, her husband had headed off with their fifteen-year-old son to the White Tower.

"A little father-son time," he had explained with a wink.

Father-son time!

"I can't see!" Anne screamed again. "I want to see the king's bed!"

Several tourists turned and looked in Anne's direction.

"Soon," Delores said to her daughter. "Just be patient, dear."

A young girl—with a head full of red hair—caught Anne's attention and pointed toward an open space near the entrance to the room.

"There!" yelled Anne as she sprinted toward the open spot.

Before her mother could react, Anne had hit the rope at full speed. The hook holding the rope to the wall disengaged immediately. The rope fell to the ground, and Anne tumbled into the exhibit space.

Henry Defessus was caught completely off-guard. One moment he was staring at the faceless mass of tourists making their way slowly through the king's bedchamber, and the next moment—complete chaos.

A small child was now jumping up and down on the king's bed. A tall, thin boy stood in the fireplace, his head in the flue. Two girls were climbing up the bedposts. A rather large woman was changing a baby's diaper on the fifteenth-century wooden table at the foot of the king's bed. Children and adults covered every square inch of the exhibit space.

Henry knew he had to act, and act fast.

"Stop that, stop that!" Henry yelled at no one in particular as he waded into the mass of children and frantic parents.

The sudden chaos also caught Art off-guard. One moment he was staring at the flat-panel display on the wall, and the next moment—complete pandemonium.

He turned just in time to see the security guard leave his post and wade into the mass of tykes, teens, tweens, toddlers, and adults.

The doorway leading to Wakefield Tower was now un-guarded.

He didn't know how Camille had managed to pull it off —but she had.

Suddenly Camille appeared from the crowd and grabbed Art by the hand, and they slipped into the stone stairwell leading to Wakefield Tower.

CHAPTER 26

10:53 a.m.
Thursday, August 14
Tower of London
London, England

At the top of the stairs they came to a small landing. Directly in front of them was the short walkway that led to Wakefield Tower. Art glanced back down the stairway. He could still hear the sounds of children screaming in the room below, but—thankfully—no one had followed Art and Camille. They made their way across the elevated walkway to a second set of stairs descending to yet another room—to Wakefield Tower.

They paused at the top of the  stairs. They could hear muffled voices in the room below.

"What do we say when we get down there?" Camille whispered. After all, they were about to barge into the middle of a group of people filming a documentary. She doubted that they would be welcomed with open arms.

"We don't give them any explanation," Art replied.

"And if they ask, we'll tell them they need to speak to the general manager."

"Who's the general manager?" Camille asked.

"Don't know, and it doesn't matter," Art said. "Hopefully that will buy us enough time to find what we need before they figure it out."

Camille nodded. If there was anyone who could bluff his way through this situation, it was Art.

With Art in the lead, they cautiously took two steps down the stairs. The voices from below became louder, more distinct.

Art paused and listened.

A man's voice directed someone to move a box to the far side of the room.

He could hear the sound of something being dragged across the room and dropped with a clank. This was followed by more discussion, but it was muted and indistinct.

With his back hard against the wall, Art took two more steps down. Camille followed close behind. Art paused once more and listened, but there was only silence. They edged down two more stairs and paused yet again at a small landing. Thick stone columns framed either side of the stairway. They squeezed into the space between one of the columns and the exterior wall.

"Well?" a deep male voice said from the room below.

"Do you even have a clue what you're doing? We brought all this high-tech equipment, and you're just staring at the wall."

And then there was another voice.

A male voice.

It was a voice that Art recognized immediately. He had heard it on several YouTube videos.

"Just be patient," the new voice said. "It's probably right in front of us."

Art turned and looked at Camille. From the shocked look on her face, it was clear that she recognized the voice as well.

CHAPTER 27

10:55 a.m.
Thursday, August 14
Tower of London
London, United Kingdom

Broderick needed time to think—to examine the room without all of the interruptions. He had a small moleskin notebook filled with sketches and ideas, but as long as Miles Davenport stayed in the room, nothing would be accomplished.

In order to maintain their cover, Davenport had insisted that they needed to bring along real camera equipment, lights, and everything else that a legitimate filmmaker would need. But they also brought along a portable x-ray machine, a thermal imaging device, a flexible probe with a minicamera, and several other instruments that could be used to see what cannot normally be seen.

The heavy black cases now sat scattered throughout the chamber. A camera and two sets of lights had been set up to give the appearance that they were actually filming in the room. Occasionally a security guard or an employee of the Tower would peek into the room. To the untrained eye, everything appeared perfectly normal. It was, however, nothing more than a charade—a carefully orchestrated plan to gain unfettered and private access to Wakefield Tower.

Broderick sighed.

There was no sense in wasting time. He had a job to do. People were counting on him—whether they knew it or not.

Broderick glanced around the room. He had spent a significant amount of time over the years in Wakefield Tower, but it seemed so different when it was not filled with tourists. The thick stone walls blocked most noise from the outside world. The room was sparsely decorated. The only piece of furniture was a small throne set into a recess at the back of the room. To the right of the throne was a stone fireplace that occupied an entire wall of the chamber. Directly opposite the throne was the small chapel where King Henry VI was allegedly murdered. Separated from the rest of the room by a brightly painted wooden screen, the chapel seemed hardly big enough for two people. The main feature of the chapel was the grouping of ornately decorated stained-glass windows—two sets of windows stacked one on top of another. Broderick found it hard to imagine the chapel as a scene of murder.

But he wasn't looking for a murderer, he was looking for—

HONK.

Davenport blew his nose for what seemed like the one hundredth time that morning. The noise reverberated throughout the small stone chamber.

HONK.

Broderick had had it. *That's it. No more.*

"I need some time alone," he said to Davenport. "Time to think."

"Not a chance," said Davenport.

"Then maybe you and your nose can figure this out," Broderick replied.

The words had just jumped out of his mouth.

Miles Davenport stared at Broderick Tinsley. Broderick could see a large vein pulsating on the side of Davenport's massive forehead, and his face had taken on a strange shade of red.

There was a long, uncomfortable pause.

"You have fifteen minutes," Davenport finally said. "I'm going to get some tea."

Footsteps.

Art could hear footsteps heading up the stairs from Wakefield Tower and in their direction. He motioned for Camille to squeeze herself as far behind the column as she could manage. Still, Art felt completely exposed.

A moment later a tall, heavyset man with a thick mustache passed within a few feet of where they stood.

Art held his breath.

Don't turn around.

The man made his way to the stairway on the opposite end of the walkway and descended toward the Medieval Palace. Camille immediately nudged past Art and started toward the stairs leading down to Wakefield Tower.

"Wait," Art whispered.

Camille turned and looked at him. "My father's by himself," she said. "This is our chance."

"What about that big guy?" Art whispered. "What was he doing with your father?"

"Why does that matter?" Camille whispered back.

Art could tell that Camille was growing impatient, and he didn't blame her. But as much as she wanted to see her father, they couldn't forget that this had all started with an ancient stolen hourglass. And Camille and Art both knew that the type of people involved in something like that could be dangerous. They couldn't afford to take any chances. Art didn't like the idea of splitting up, but he also didn't like the idea of the large man with the mustache unexpectedly returning to find them both in Wakefield Tower.

"Because whatever your father is involved in," Art said, "he's not alone. You go after your father. I'm following the big guy."

Camille paused for a second, nodded, and then started to descend the stairs.

CHAPTER 28

10:56 a.m.
Thursday, August 14
Tower of London
London, England

Alone. Finally.

Thank goodness.

Broderick Tinsley turned on the large portable lights set up in the middle of the room. The lights hummed slightly as they warmed up. Within seconds, the entire room was bathed in bright light. Every crack, every corner, every detail of the room, was now exposed to view and examination.

Broderick opened his notebook and started going over his notes. It had taken him much longer than he had expected to break the first part of the riddle: *In weak field whence youth depart'd.*

However, once he realized it was an anagram, it all fell into place.

Wakefield Tower.

The boy king — the youth.

King Henry VI.

There was no question that the professor was where he was supposed to be.

Broderick made his way over to the small chapel on the south side of the chamber. He stepped past the wooden screen and into the small room. The morning light filtered through the two rows of stained-glass windows in front of him and lightly painted the tiled floor and stone walls in pale shades of red, green, yellow, purple, and blue. In the middle of the floor — among the ornately decorated rust-colored tiles — was a single white tile. Upon that tile was inscribed a short but poignant memorial:

> *By Tradition*
> *Henry VI died here*
> *May 21st 1471*

The small room — simple as it may have been — was mesmerizing.

Three made one ye sign impart'd.

The next clue.

Break it down, Broderick told himself. *Keep it simple.*

Three made one.

Three what?

Broderick glanced down at his notes. Henry VI had served as king during three different periods — twice in England and once in France. He had been, according to legend, murdered by Richard III. His coat of arms was made up of three sections, not four. And on the coat of arms were three groups of three fleur-de-lis. The small chapel had three sides, and there were three windows in each row of stained-glass windows in the chapel.

Broderick sighed.

Finding the number three associated with Henry VI or Wakefield Tower had not been a problem. Finding the correct association, however, was another story.

Broderick had hoped to find some evidence of the king's coat of arms in the chapel. The coat of arms had seemed the most likely candidate for the next clue in the riddle: one heraldic shield composed of three sections, not the usual four. But the chamber—and the chapel in particular—offered no hint of the symbols from the coat of arms.

Perhaps the stained-glass windows?

In theory, the windows—two rows of three windows each—had also seemed like a logical suspect for the next clue. But one look at the stained-glass windows shattered any illusion that the windows harbored anything of interest. The windows were a jumbled mess of colors and shapes—formless and without meaning.

He had to be missing something.

Broderick started thumbing through his notes when he heard the shuffle of feet behind him on the stone floor of the chamber.

He shook his head in frustration.

Oh, c'mon, he thought. It had not even been five minutes, and Davenport had already returned.

"I need more time alone," he said without looking up from his notebook.

"And I want answers," a voice responded. It was not Davenport.

No, Broderick thought. *Not now.*

Not here.

The security guard was finally getting things back under control in the king's bedchamber as Art slipped back through the room. The velvet rope had been put back in place, and the crowds were once more circulating through the room in counterclockwise fashion.

Art immediately spotted the man with the mustache on the far side of the room.

Wow, thought Art. *He sure doesn't look like a documentary filmmaker.*

The man was huge. He towered over everyone in the room, and his neck was the size of a tree trunk.

Art tensed up immediately.

What have we gotten ourselves into?

Art glanced back at the hallway leading to Wakefield Tower. He briefly considered calling Camille and telling her that she needed to get as far away from her father as possible. But Art knew exactly what her response would be — the same response he would have given if it had been his father.

He had no choice but to do what he had told Camille he was going to do—follow the large man with the mustache. Art slipped into the crowd leaving the king's bedchamber and followed the man as he made his way toward the exit.

CHAPTER 29

Camille stood at the entrance to the tower, her arms folded and a scowl on her face.

"You can't be here," insisted Broderick. His voice was barely above a whisper.

Camille didn't budge. She was no longer worried about her father and whatever he had gotten involved in — she was furious with him. He had abandoned her — again. He had lied to her. He had disappointed her. She wanted answers.

"Why are you here?" she demanded.

"Keep it down," Broderick said. "Someone will hear you."

"I don't care if someone hears me," said Camille. "You were supposed to be at the airport yesterday. You were supposed to meet me there. You didn't."

Broderick stepped out of the chapel and over to a doorway on the opposite side of the room. There was an exit sign above the door. "This door will take you down through Wakefield Tower and back outside," he said. "If you run into

123

anyone—and I mean anyone—just tell them you got lost. Don't tell anyone your name."

Camille didn't budge. "What are you looking for?" she asked. "And don't lie to me—I know all about the hourglass and the riddle."

The blood drained from Broderick's face. "This is a lot more complicated and dangerous than you can ever imagine," he said. "You have to go—it's not safe here."

"Not safe?" said Camille. She glanced around the room. "We're completely alone. I want to know what's going on, and I'm not leaving until you tell me."

"You don't understand," her father replied.

"I told you I know about the stolen hourglass," she said. "And the riddle."

"That's not it," Broderick said.

"Then what don't I understand?" Camille demanded.

Art followed the man down the stairs to the open walkway where he and Camille had first entered the Medieval Palace. The man turned right at the bottom of the stairs and headed farther into the vast grounds of the Tower of London. Art took a quick glance at his guide map to get his bearings. They were in the area of the Tower known as the Water Lane—a long stone pathway that ran parallel to the River Thames, which was located on the far side of the high stone wall to his right. The crowd had thinned out somewhat in the lane, which made it easier to follow the man. However, Art realized that this also made it easier for him to be seen. He dropped back a bit farther to avoid detection.

The man passed beneath the arched walkway that ran between the wall to his right and the round building on his left—Wakefield Tower. It was the same walkway he and Camille had been standing on just moments ago. Art glanced toward Wakefield Tower. Camille was somewhere in that building.

Art had a sudden feeling of guilt. Camille was only twelve years old, and he had just helped her sneak into an ancient stone fortress with no idea what she would find inside. What if her father was a thief, or worse? How much did Camille really know about her father? They had exchanged some emails, texts, and letters. They had Skyped a few times. But that was it. Art knew that it would have been impossible to stop her from going into the tower, but he could have at least tried.

Art shook it off. He could worry about his failures as a friend some other time. Right now he had a job to do.

Following at a safe distance, Art watched as the man passed another round tower near the end of the lane. Unexpectedly, the man took an immediate left past the tower and disappeared out of sight. Art hustled to catch up. He reached the end of the lane and—staying as close to the round tower as possible—peeked around the wall and in the direction in which the man had disappeared. Art was surprised to find a large courtyard filled with tourists.

Art looked from one side of the courtyard to the other. To his left and across a wide green lawn was a massive tower made of white stone — it was four stories high with turrets on each corner. It looked ancient. To his right was a large red brick building, much more modern in appearance. Art scanned the crowd for the large man. He was nowhere to be seen.

Art pounded his fist against the stone wall of the Water Lane.

I've lost him.

Camille stood her ground. She was not moving until her father explained what was going on. She had spent years wondering about her father. Who was he? What was he like? Why had he abandoned her and her mother? The past few months had offered answers to some of those questions, and she wasn't about to just walk away now.

Broderick Tinsley sighed and turned to her. "What you don't understand," he said, "is that you are about to place you, your mom, and your friend in grave danger."

CHAPTER 30

11:01 a.m.
Thursday, August 14
Tower of London
London, England

Grave danger?

Something in her father's voice brought Camille's train of thought to a sudden stop.

She had been so caught up in her own emotions that she had not taken the time to see what was right in front of her. Her father looked exhausted. He had not shaved, and she could see dark bags under his eyes. But it was his voice that really caught her attention. He wasn't angry or upset that she had found him. He was worried. He was scared.

"I just wanted to see you," she said.

The tears—held back by the anger—finally started to flow.

Broderick Tinsley could barely speak. "I'm so sorry," he said, his voice cracking. "I had no choice."

There!

Art caught a brief glimpse of the man just as he was

entering the large red brick building to his right. Art hurried across the courtyard toward the entrance to the building. A sign hanging in front identified it as the New Armouries Café.

Art hurried up the steps and into the restaurant.

Camille wiped the tears from her eyes. "What do you mean, you had no choice?"

Broderick glanced nervously at his watch and then retrieved a large brown envelope from his satchel. He pulled something out of the envelope and handed it to Camille. It was a photograph of Camille and her mother at a local bookstore near their home in Washington, DC. It had been taken from afar. It felt intrusive, as if someone had been spying on them.

Camille was confused. "What's this all about?" she asked.

"The photo is a reminder," Broderick replied.

He held up the brown envelope. "It's filled with reminders," he said.

"Reminders of what?" Camille asked.

"Reminders of what matters to me," he replied.

Art stepped into the restaurant and glanced around. The décor was bright and modern—a stark contrast to everything else within the Tower complex. He caught sight of the man at the coffee bar on the far side of the restaurant. Art moved around to the right side of the restaurant and selected a Coke Zero from a cooler. There were several cashiers located throughout the restaurant. Art found the nearest cashier and paid for his soda, all the time keeping a close eye on the man. The large man—now holding a steaming cup of tea—sat down in a booth. Another row of booths ran parallel to the row in which the man was sitting, and a short wall with a frosted glass screen on top separated the two rows. Art casually made his way toward the front of the restaurant and then turned down the row of booths on the side opposite the row in which the man was sitting. The booth immediately adjacent to the man's booth was unoccupied. Art slipped into it and slunk low in the seat. He could see the silhouette of the man through the frosted-glass partition. Art squeezed as close as he could to the wall that separated the booths.

"My life has always been about history," said Broderick Tinsley. "It defines who we are, where we have been, and where we will go. I teach history because it is important and because it matters. I believe history belongs to all of us. But there are people who simply want to sell history to the highest bidder, and they will do anything to get what they want."

"Anything?" asked Camille.

"Yes," replied Broderick. "Even hurt those whom I care about."

Camille looked down at the photograph in her hand and realized in an instant what had occurred. The photographs in the brown envelope were not simply reminders, they were threats.

"That big man—the one with the mustache," Camille said. "He gave you these photos, didn't he? You have to do what he says or . . ."

Broderick nodded. "Or else."

"But why you?" she asked.

"Because he believes my knowledge of English history will help him find what he is looking for," Broderick replied. "He needed an expert, and he chose me. He knew all about the history of the hourglass. He suspected it was something more than what it appeared to be, but its secrets eluded him. I helped him uncover those secrets."

"The riddle," Camille said.

Broderick Tinsley nodded. "Yes," he replied. "The riddle—hidden in plain sight for centuries—is the key. "

"And what is he looking for?" Camille asked.

"A missing piece of history," her father responded. "He believes the riddle will lead us to the location of an object known as Llywelyn's coronet."

"Never heard of it," Camille replied.

"Most people haven't," her father said. "A coronet is

a type of crown, and it was part of the Crown Jewels of England until it disappeared almost four hundred years ago."

"It must have been pretty fancy," Camille said. She imagined a large elaborate crown filled with jewels and made of gold.

"To the contrary," her father said. "It was very simple —maybe even just a large ring made of iron."

"No jewels?" Camille asked.

"No jewels," her father responded.

"No gold?"

"No gold."

Camille was confused. "Then why would this guy go through all this trouble to get a crown made of iron? I mean, I know it's old and all that, but . . . c'mon. No gold or jewels or anything like that? Why would he want that?"

"It's not valuable because of what it is made of," Broderick said, "but because of who is rumored to have worn it."

"A king?" Camille asked. That much seemed obvious.

Broderick nodded. "A king named Arthur."

Art put his ear to the wall separating the booths. Moments later he heard the distinctive clicking sound of buttons being pushed on a phone. The man was either texting or making a call.

Art closed his eyes and listened intently, fervently wishing the man was calling someone and there would be something to overhear.

There was a moment of silence, and then the man with the mustache spoke.

"It's me," he said.

Another pause.

"I always find what I am looking for," the man said. "You'll have it sitting on your mantel by the end of the week."

Another pause.

"You paid for the best," the man said. "And that's what you get."

Another pause.

The man chuckled.

"My assistant?" he said from the other booth. "Do you really want to know what will happen to him when this is all over?"

Another pause.

"Tomorrow," the man said. "You'll have it tomorrow."

There was a click. The call had ended.

Art had a knot in his stomach.

He still had no idea what Camille's father had gotten himself into or what they were looking for, but it seemed abundantly clear that it was not going to end well for Professor Tinsley.

Art pulled out his phone to text Camille. Maybe she could warn her father.

Art started to type out a message and then paused. He needed to get Camille out of Wakefield Tower—that much was clear. This adventure had suddenly become very serious. But it wouldn't take Camille more than a few moments to get out of the tower. And maybe if he followed the big guy a little longer, he might find a way to get Professor Tinsley out of this mess. Art could simply continue to follow the man and wait to alert Camille once they were closer.

CHAPTER 31

11:07 a.m.
Thursday, August 14
Tower of London
London, England

Art heard the large man getting up from his table. The man was now in a position to see over the partition and into Art's booth. Art hastily bent over his cell phone and pretended he was playing a game. As far as he could tell, the man had not noticed that he was sitting there. From the corner of his eye, Art saw the man head toward the front of the restaurant. Art counted to ten and then slipped out of the booth. He caught sight of the man just as he turned the corner into the foyer of the restaurant. Art waited until the man was out of sight and then headed for the exit.

It took a moment for what her father had just said to sink in.

"Wait," Camille said, "the riddle on the hourglass leads to . . . King Arthur's crown?"

Her father nodded.

"*The* King Arthur?" Camille said. "I didn't think he was real."

"Not as we know him from the movies and books," Broderick replied, "but many people believe that there was a real person on which the stories are based."

"So what happened to the crown?" asked Camille.

"It was brought to London centuries ago," her father explained, "and it was rumored that only the true ruler of England could wear Arthur's crown."

Camille could see why the large man would want the treasure. Who wouldn't want to own King Arthur's crown? She imagined it was worth a fortune. She had plenty of questions about what was going on, but there was one particular question that she couldn't get off her mind.

"So what does all of this have to do with King Henry VI?" she asked.

Broderick checked his watch again. He knew that he didn't have time to waste. But even though he had known his daughter for only a month or two, and their communications had been limited, it was clear that she was determined, fearless, smart—and that she would not be easily rushed along without an explanation.

"Henry VI may not have been a very good king," Broderick said, "but the people of England adored him. He was viewed almost as a saint after he died. And if you were going to choose someone to protect something as important as King Arthur's crown, why not ask a saint to do it?"

Broderick glanced anxiously around. Davenport would be back any minute. "Unfortunately," he continued, "this is where it may all end if I can't figure out the second part of the first line of the clue: 'Three made one ye sign impart'd.'"

"Then it's a good thing I'm here to help," Camille replied.

Art once again counted to ten before turning the corner into the foyer.

Be careful, he cautioned himself.

He stepped into the foyer. It was empty—just a wooden bench, a sign pointing toward the cafeteria, and a maintenance closet. He glanced outside, but there was no sign of the man.

Where did he go? Art wondered.

Art did not have long to ponder where or how the man had disappeared.

Art felt someone grab his arm, and suddenly he was jerked backwards into darkness.

CHAPTER 32

Camille stepped into the small chapel and looked around.

The stained-glass windows immediately drew her attention. They were the predominant feature in the room —two rows of three windows.

"I know what you're thinking," said Broderick. "But it's not the windows—there's nothing there. Just a bunch of abstract shapes and colors in stained glass."

Her father was right. The windows were a disorganized mess.

"I thought stained-glass windows usually had—you know—pictures and stuff in them?" asked Camille. "Like kings and dragons."

Camille had visited the Washington National Cathedral in DC and seen all of the massive stained-glass windows. They were filled with images and patterns. There was nothing random about them, unlike the ones in Wakefield Tower. She walked directly up to the middle window and ran her hand across it. She could feel how the morning sun had warmed it up, and she could see small air bubbles trapped in the ancient colored glass.

She wished Art were here.

He could solve this puzzle, she thought.

Camille paused.

But he's not here, a little voice inside her said.

It's just you.

Solve it yourself.

Art was shoved up against a wall. He caught a brief glimpse of the foyer just before the door to the maintenance closet slammed shut.

It was now pitch-black.

Something—someone—had a grip on his right forearm. It felt like the bones in his arm were going to be crushed. His heart was beating a mile a minute.

"Who are you?" Art asked.

No answer.

He could now hear someone breathing in the dark.

Suddenly the light in the maintenance room flickered on.

Staring down at him was the large man with the mustache.

He was even bigger—and much more intimidating—up close.

Art glanced down at the hand wrapped around his

forearm. It was massive, with fingers the size and color of large Italian sausages. And then there was the man's face. He had small scars on his forehead, and his left ear was a mass of purplish scar tissue. His nose had a strange leftward bend to it, and his mustache drooped down over his mouth. His face looked as if it had been put through a meat grinder.

"You've been following me since I left the Medieval Palace," the man said. His voice was deep and flat. There was no emotion. "And I want to know why."

He tightened his grip on Art's forearm. A bolt of pain shot up Art's arm. He was losing all feeling in his hand.

"Answer me," the man said, "or I'll snap your forearm in half."

Art winced, but he refused to cry out. He knew that would make matters only worse. He needed to find some way to explain what he was doing.

The man tightened his grip yet again.

"Answer me," he demanded.

Art closed his eyes. The pain was unbearable.

And then it occurred to him.

Wigan.

CHAPTER 33

11:09 a.m.
Thursday, August 14
Tower of London
London, England

"Wigan," Art grunted through clenched teeth.

"Wigan?" asked the large man.

Art nodded. "Wigan," he repeated.

"What's that supposed to mean?" the man asked.

Art held up his cell phone with his free hand. "I wanted a picture," he said.

The large man took the cell phone from Art and squeezed his forearm tighter. Art could no longer feel his right hand.

"Why did you want my picture?" the man demanded.

"W-Wigan," sputtered Art. "You play for Wigan, don't you?"

The man loosened his grip on Art's forearm ever so slightly.

"What are you talking about?" he asked.

"Rugby," Art said. "You're Thomas Bloodworth, aren't you? You play fullback for the Wigan Warriors. I was watching you on television yesterday."

It was all Art could think of under the circumstances. He had spent much of the previous morning watching rugby on his hotel room TV. Rugby was like football but without the pads and helmets, and rugby players were all pretty big guys. Wigan was the first team that popped into his head, and Thomas Bloodworth was the only player he could remember.

"Rugby?" the man said.

He loosened his grip on Art's forearm a little bit more. Art could feel the blood flowing back into his hand.

"I'm a big fan," said Art. "I just wanted a photo to prove I saw you. My dad will never believe me."

The large man looked Art directly in the eyes.

"I've never played rugby," the man said as he finally released his grip on Art's arm.

The man snapped Art's cell phone in two and dropped it into a nearby pail of dirty mop water. He then opened the door to the maintenance room and turned to face Art.

"You shouldn't follow people around," he said. "You could get hurt."

He stepped outside and shut the door behind him.

Art dropped to his knees and held his right forearm tight against his chest. His arm throbbed with pain. He was sure that it was broken.

He took several deep breaths.

Calm down, he told himself.

He could worry about his arm later—he had to get Camille out of the tower and was kicking himself for not heading directly there after he'd overheard the big man on the phone.

Art glanced over at the mop bucket into which his cell phone had been dropped.

Calling or texting Camille was now completely out of the question. He instantly regretted not contacting her when he'd had the chance.

His only option was to get to Wakefield Tower and warn her before the large man got there. Art reached into his pocket with his left hand and pulled out the map of the Tower of London. There were two routes back to the Medieval Palace. Art assumed that the large man would take the same route he had taken to the restaurant—between the walls of the inner and outer wards. It was a more direct route, but it would be crowded with tourists entering the Tower of London. The other route was around the White Tower and then down the stairs to a gate in the wall of the inner ward. This route was less direct but more wide open and less likely to be packed tightly with tourists. Directly across from the gate was the entrance to the Medieval Palace. The gate, Art noted with a chill, passed through a structure in the wall called the Bloody Tower.

Great. I have to make it through the Bloody Tower.

Art stood up and walked over to the door of the

maintenance room. He cracked it open just enough to peek outside. In the distance he could see the large man. He had a head start, but it was not insurmountable.

Art made his way to the front door of the building and looked across the plaza to his left.

The man had almost reached the passageway between the inner and outer wards.

Art took a deep breath. His arm continued to pulsate with pain.

He watched as the man turned the corner and disappeared out of sight.

Without a moment's hesitation, Art burst out of the restaurant and started sprinting toward the rear of the White Tower.

CHAPTER 34

11:10 a.m.
Thursday, August 14
Tower of London
London, England

Camille stood in front of the stained-glass windows.

Three windows.

Three made one.

She moved to the window farthest to her left.

"We don't have time for this," Broderick Tinsley said. "You have to leave."

Camille didn't respond. She moved to the window farthest to her right and ran her hand along the left edge of the window. Her fingers lingered over an ancient iron hinge. She looked up. An identical hinge was attached near the top of the window along the same edge.

Could it really be that simple?

Art held his right arm as tight as he could against his chest as he ran, but the pain was becoming increasingly difficult to ignore. Each step was agonizing. He gritted his teeth and kept running.

Within moments, he had reached the rear of the White Tower. He turned left and sprinted across the open plaza behind the massive stone structure. To his right was the large building that housed the Crown Jewels. A crowd of tourists was lined up waiting to get in to see the jewels. A guard yelled for Art to slow down. Art threw his arm up to acknowledge the guard but kept running.

Upon reaching the far side of the plaza, Art turned left. He stopped for a second to get his bearings and catch his breath. Directly in front of him and at the end of a cobblestone path was the Bloody Tower. The gate was fewer than two hundred feet away. He had more than enough time to get ahead of the man.

Art sprinted toward the gate and bounded down a set of wide stairs built into the stone path.

A hundred feet to go.

He could now see the crowds streaming through the passageway on the far side of the gate. He would be in the Medieval Palace within seconds.

Fifty feet to go.

Another set of stairs. Art hit them at full speed.

Twenty-five feet to go.

He could now see the entrance to the Medieval Palace. He was almost there.

And then, suddenly, a wall of dark blue and red appeared between him and the gate. He stopped quickly, almost losing his balance in the process.

"Hold on there," the man standing in front of him said as he put his hand on Art's shoulder to steady him. "No running on the grounds."

Art looked up at the middle-aged man standing in front of him. He was dressed in the distinctive uniform of the Yeoman Warder—the Beefeater. The man wore a long coat with a matching belt. Embroidered on the front of his coat —in extraordinarily large script—were the initials "ER." On his head was a flat-brimmed hat. The man had a neatly trimmed gray beard and wore a pair of oval-shaped glasses. He looked Art straight in the eyes.

"No running on the grounds," the man repeated. "Is that understood?" His tone was calm, measured, and completely authoritative.

Art nodded. "I'm sorry," he said. "I just need to get . . ."

At that moment, on the far side of the gate—fewer than fifteen feet away—he saw the large man pass by.

He was too late. The man would be inside the Medieval Palace in a matter of seconds.

"Now," the Yeoman Warder said, "where might you be heading in such a hurry?"

"Nowhere," Art replied. "Nowhere."

CHAPTER 35

Camille smiled.

She could feel the puzzle pieces falling into place. Was this how Art felt when he solved a clue? She turned to her father to explain what she had found, but the look on his face stopped her in her tracks.

His face had turned white.

"What is it?" she asked.

"Footsteps," he whispered. "And they're not far away."

Someone was coming. Whoever it was would be in the tower in mere seconds.

Broderick grabbed Camille by the arm and dragged her toward the exit at the far side of the room. There was no time for niceties or goodbyes. A set of spiral stairs descended into darkness.

"Follow the stairs and look for the exit sign," he whispered. "You'll be safe."

"Wait," Camille said. "We need to—"

"No," said Broderick. His voice was firm and determined. "Go — now."

Camille could hear the footsteps getting louder. Whoever was coming would be in the chamber in a heartbeat.

"The hinges!" she whispered as she turned to head down the stairs. "It's the hinges!"

Camille made her way quickly down the stone spiral staircase.

No one seemed to be following her. She was alone.

Hinge.

She hoped her father would understand what she'd been jabbering about as she had left the tower. If he did understand, then she needed to find a way out of Wakefield Tower as quickly as possible.

And then there was Art. She had no idea where he was.

Camille texted him: "Where r u?" She waited a moment, but there was no response.

Camille continued down the stairs until she reached a small chamber. The room was cool and dark. The thick stone walls cut off any sounds from the bustling world outside. Overhead spotlights illuminated a series of exhibits against the wall to her left. A small sign at the bottom of the stairs explained that the room contained examples of torture devices previously used in the Tower of London.

A shudder went up Camille's spine. *Great — a torture*

chamber. She was convinced that if there was a room in the entire Tower complex that was haunted, this had to be it.

The sooner she was out of this room, the better.

Camille spied an illuminated exit sign on the far side of the room and sprinted toward it.

Art stepped through the gate beneath the Bloody Tower and into the passageway between the walls of the inner and outer wards. Directly in front of him was the stairway leading to the Medieval Palace—the same stairway that he and Camille had used earlier that morning. The large man was nowhere to be seen. He had obviously made his way back into the palace and was probably already back in Wakefield Tower.

Art needed time to think. He noticed a small alley adjacent to the round stone building to his left—the bottom of Wakefield Tower. From there he could observe anyone leaving the Medieval Palace. Art made his way over to the alley and out of the rush of tourists pouring around him.

He leaned against the wall of the tower and rubbed his arm. The throbbing pain had turned into a dull ache. His forearm was red and swollen.

He had no way of getting in contact with Camille. His cell phone—well, what was left of his cell phone—was sitting at the bottom of a bucket full of dirty mop water. Camille could, he realized, be perfectly safe. She may have left the tower long ago. But without his phone, he had no way of knowing where she was or what she was doing.

Whatever was going on inside Wakefield Tower, it was clearly not the filming of a documentary. He had no choice —he had to tell the security guard what was happening and ask him to check on Camille. Art understood what that would mean. Everything they were doing would be discovered. His father and Camille's mother would be furious. But he knew he had no choice. He could not take the chance that Camille was still in the tower.

Art took one last look around, hopeful that he would spot Camille leaving the Medieval Palace or strolling along the passageway. No such luck.

All right, then, let's do this.

The tap on his shoulder made him jump two feet in the air.

"Why didn't you answer my text?" the voice behind him asked.

Art turned to find Camille staring at him.

"Camille!" Art exclaimed. "You're safe!"

Camille pointed to a door at the end of the alley. "That's an exit from the bottom floor of Wakefield Tower," she said.

"What about your dad?" Art asked. "Did you talk to him?"

Ignoring Art's question, Camille looked up at the exterior wall of Wakefield Tower. "Dang," she said as she pushed past Art. "Wrong side."

Art hustled to catch up. "What do you mean, 'wrong side'?"

Camille sprinted out of the alley, turned left, and headed for the opposite side of the tower. She stopped in the middle of the passageway on the far side and stared up at the exterior of the building. Directly above her were six stained-glass windows—two rows of three.

"C'mon," she said to herself. "You can do it."

Art caught up with Camille. "What are you talking about?" he asked.

Camille pointed up. "The windows," she said excitedly. "The stained glass was the key to the riddle—can you believe it? I solved it. Or at least I think I did. I just sort of thought, *Hey, hinges.* And then there were footsteps, and I had to leave. But it's the windows."

Art looked up at the stained-glass windows. They glowed with color, which struck Art as odd. It was as if they were illuminated from the inside of the building.

"What about the windows?" he asked.

Camille turned to Art. "Hinges," Camille said. "I'm waiting on my dad to see the hinges."

CHAPTER 36

11:12 a.m.

Thursday, August 14

Tower of London

London, England

Hinges?

Broderick stood in the middle of the chamber and stared at the stained-glass windows.

What is Camille talking about?

"Well?" Davenport demanded. "Have you solved the riddle?" He glanced at his watch. "We're running out of time," he said. "We need to get moving."

A broad grin broke out on Broderick's face.

"Of course!" he exclaimed. "Moving! Hinges!"

Broderick rushed over to the stained-glass windows. He went first to the window on the left. On the side of the window — barely perceptible — was a small latch. Broderick reached up and pulled on it. It didn't budge, which was not particularly surprising since it had probably been a couple hundred years since it was last opened.

He motioned toward Miles Davenport. "Come here," he said. "I need this opened."

Davenport walked over to the window and examined

the ancient latch. He reached up, took the small iron lever in his hand, and pulled down. The latch released, and the window opened ever so slightly.

Broderick made his way over to the window on the far right side of the chapel and pointed at an identical latch on that window. "This one also," he said.

Davenport made his way over to the window on the right side and opened it as well.

"What about the middle window?" Davenport asked.

"It doesn't open," Broderick replied confidently.

"I hope you have a good explanation for all of this," Davenport said.

"Three made one," Broderick said. He then turned to the window on the far left and opened it wide. He folded it over the middle window. It fit perfectly.

Davenport gasped. An image had suddenly appeared in the stained glass when the windows overlapped. It was a man in some sort of semicircle. He seemed to be gesturing with his right arm. Beneath the image were the letters S, T, and R. But the image was clearly incomplete.

Broderick went to the window on the far right and opened it wide as well. It too folded neatly over the middle window.

No one spoke.

It was incredible. Individually each window was simply a random assortment of oddly shaped pieces of glass — abstract and indistinct. But layered on top of one another, the windows revealed an unmistakable image — a picture of a man sowing seeds in a pasture. And beneath the image was a single word: SATOR.

Broderick turned to Davenport.

"In weak field whence youth depart'd, three made one ye sign impart'd," he said.

"Yes!" Camille exclaimed.

Art stared up at the stained-glass windows. He could not believe what he had just witnessed. A moment ago there had been six stained-glass windows, each a jumble of odd shapes and colors. And then the stained-glass windows on the bottom row had, as if by magic, changed completely. The left and right windows had simply disappeared, and the middle window had transformed from an abstract assemblage into a distinct picture — an image of a man casting seeds in a field. And beneath the image a set of symbols: Я O T A Ƨ.

Я O T A Ƨ?

And then it hit him — they were looking at the back of the windows. Those weren't strange symbols or some sort of ancient language. They were letters, just reversed and backwards.

Reversed and in proper order, the letters spelled . . . SATOR?

What does that mean?

Art glanced over at Camille, who was busily snapping photos of the window with her cell phone.

In all the excitement over the windows, Art had almost forgotten what he'd heard back at the restaurant.

"Your father?" he asked. "Is he all right?"

Camille nodded excitedly. "Yes," she said. "He's being forced to solve the riddle on the hourglass — there was this envelope full of pictures. And that guy you followed — the big guy — he's the one doing all of this. And then I helped my dad with the first clue. I mean, I thought, *Hey, if Art can do it, why can't I do it?* And then I just did it. I just saw the hinges and thought, *Three makes one.* You know, and because there were no kings or dragons."

"Hinges? Kings and dragons?"

"Long story," Camille said. "But as soon as my dad solves the rest of the riddle and finds King Arthur's crown, everything will be back to normal."

Wait, what?

King Arthur's crown?

Art knew it would take some time to decipher exactly what had just happened — and why. But he could not forget what had happened at the restaurant. The cold, dark stare of the large man, and his aching arm reminded him that this was not a game.

* * *

Camille could see it in Art's eyes. Something was wrong. He clearly did not share her relief over finding her father.

And that's when she noticed his right arm. It was red and swollen. Art held it tight against his chest. It was clearly causing him a lot of pain.

"Art!" she gasped. "What happened?"

"I had a run-in with the guy who's in the tower with your father," he replied. "Not good."

Camille reached out to touch Art's arm. He jerked it back instinctively. She could see the grimace on his face as his arm moved.

"We need to get that checked out," she said. "It could be broken."

Art nodded. "I think it is," he replied. "But we have a bigger problem—I think your father's in a whole lot of danger."

CHAPTER 37

Camille sat on a bench overlooking the River Thames—a wide expanse of briskly flowing gray-green water that flowed through the middle of London. Directly behind her was the Tower of London. On the far side of the river was a large silver building shaped like an egg. It was modern, as were many of the buildings surrounding it. The contrast with the ancient fortress behind her was startling.

As weird as it seemed, it had been a relief to find out that her father had not run away because of her. To the contrary, he was actually protecting her. But Camille's relief had turned to concern when she learned what Art had overheard in the restaurant. And her concern had turned to alarm when Art described what had happened to his arm. Whatever plans the large man had for her father, it seemed clear that simply letting him return to his post as a professor was not among them.

And then there was the image from the windows. A man throwing seeds in a field and the word SATOR. A quick Internet search revealed that the word *sator* was Latin. It meant someone who planted seeds—a sower, the image from the stained glass.

So the first sign was a sower.

Great, Camille thought. *That really clears things up.*

She had explained to Art that the riddle might lead to King Arthur's crown. He had been as surprised as she had been, but he had not been surprised at the lengths to which someone might go to find a treasure like that.

"Here you go."

Camille looked up. It was Art. He handed her a Coke and sat down beside her. She noticed that although he had bought himself a soda, he wasn't drinking it. Rather, he was keeping the cold drink pressed against his right forearm and had winced in pain as he sat down.

"You need to see a doctor," she said. She was worried about her father, but it was clear that her friend was in pain. Maybe it was time to tell someone what was happening.

Art shook his head. "There's no time. The next clue is at Windsor Castle. Broderick and the treasure hunter will be heading there as soon as they get packed up. We need to get there first."

"He's not a treasure hunter," Camille said. "The big guy is a thief. He's trying to steal something that doesn't belong to him—and he's forcing my dad to help."

Art nodded. "You're right," he said. "He's a thief."

"You know that my mom will freak when she finds out

what we're doing," said Camille. "We'll be grounded for the rest of our lives."

"Probably," replied Art. "But what if we don't go? What if we tell your mom what's going on? Even if she believes us, what will happen? She notifies the police? Can you imagine how that will go? A story about a stolen hourglass? King Henry VI? Messages hidden in stained glass? King Arthur's crown?"

Art was right. It was unbelievable.

"And even if we did convince them to believe us," he continued, "how long will that take? And what happens to your father if the big guy figures out that his plan's been busted?"

Art held up his injured arm. "I know what that guy's capable of," he said, then paused.

"I don't have a plan," he finally said. "But we have to find whatever they're looking for before they do. That's the only leverage we have. Windsor's less than a half hour away by train. We can use our rail passes to get there and back by this afternoon. We have to do it."

Camille did not immediately respond. She gazed out across the river. Tourists meandered around them, posing for pictures and enjoying the day.

"Why are you doing this?" she finally asked.

"What do you mean?" Art replied. He seemed genuinely surprised by her question.

"You don't even know my dad," she said. "Heck, I'm

still trying to figure out why I'm doing this—I barely know him."

Camille pointed at Art's arm. "You're hurt, and you need to go to a doctor. And whatever happens, we're probably going to end up in a whole lot of trouble."

Art nodded. "Yep, we're going to be in a bunch of trouble."

"So why?" Camille asked. "Why not just call your dad and get this over with?"

Art shrugged. "You've always been there for me," he said. "I guess it's just my turn to help you."

CHAPTER 38

1:20 p.m.
Thursday, August 14
Traveling to Windsor, England

The train ride to Windsor was taking longer than expected, and Art worried that Professor Tinsley and the thief might beat them to the castle. But what was the sense in worrying about something over which he had no control? He needed to focus. If they had a little extra time to kill, then it was best to put it to good use. They still needed to solve the second part of the riddle.

Whence youth now sleeps three saints reside, ye second signs held by her side.

One thing was clear—if the clue from Wakefield Tower was any indication, solving the second part of the riddle would not be an easy task. With the help of Eunice they had solved the first part of the second line—"whence youth now sleeps." Henry VI—the baby king—may have died at Wakefield Tower, but he now slept for eternity in a tomb at St George's Chapel at Windsor Castle. And even though it was incredibly helpful knowing where the next clue would be found, Art also knew that they faced an uphill battle once they arrived in Windsor. He had visited Windsor Castle on several occasions with his father and understood that the term "chapel" was misleading. St George's Chapel was a large and majestic building with hundreds of stained-glass windows. Located on the grounds of Windsor Castle, it had served the British monarchy for almost a thousand years. And Henry VI was not alone in his sleep at St George's. A long list of British monarchs shared Henry VI's final resting place, including Henry VIII, perhaps the most famous of the British monarchs. While that was fascinating from a historical perspective, it also meant that there were large sections of St George's Chapel that were completely off-limits to tourists.

Art had borrowed Camille's phone and Googled the words "three saints Windsor." The search had produced almost five million results. He had skimmed through the first few pages of results but realized quickly that it was a useless endeavor. The best place to start when they reached the chapel, he finally concluded, was with the one part of the clue that they did understand—Henry VI's tomb. It seemed that the answer to the rest of the riddle would be found only within the chapel itself, where the king was buried.

CHAPTER 39

1:30 p.m.
Thursday, August 14
Windsor & Eton Central Railway Station
Windsor, England

The sunshine of the morning had given way to gray skies as the train arrived in Windsor. Camille and Art made their way down the platform and into the crowded railway station. The station was located in the center of town and featured all sorts of interesting shops, outdoor vendors, and restaurants. Art stopped at a small souvenir stand just inside the station.

"What are you doing?" asked Camille. "We need to get to the castle."

Art shook his head. "I can't go into town looking like this," he said. "If they've beat us here, the big guy will spot me immediately. He knows what I look like."

Art wore a bright blue T-shirt and his hair had turned a light blond from all the summer sun. "I suppose you're right," Camille said.

Art grabbed a long-sleeved black T-shirt that read "I Love Windsor" and a dark brown English flat cap from the sales racks. He paid the cart vendor, slipped the black T-shirt over his shirt, and placed the cap on his head.

Camille smiled. "It's not the best disguise," she said. "But at least it's different."

They made their way through the rest of the station and then exited beneath the arched brick entrance into town. Directly in front of them were the massive stone walls that surrounded Windsor Castle. St George's Chapel was located almost directly on the other side of the walls.

A large sign at the entrance provided a map of Windsor Castle. It was composed of three sections — a lower ward, a middle ward, and an upper ward. The upper ward contained the royal apartments — the place where the queen, her family, and guests stayed when they were at Windsor. The middle ward of the castle was primarily defined by a large round tower that sat on top of a small hill. Centuries ago, it was the place where a king or queen would go if the castle was attacked. But it was the lower ward that interested Camille and Art. The primary architectural feature of the lower ward was a towering stone structure — St George's Chapel.

Camille and Art entered the castle in the middle ward and made their way down the sloping pathway toward St George's Chapel.

"Do you think they're already here?" asked Camille.

Art—who was wondering the same thing—carefully examined the throngs of tourists making their way around the castle grounds. He was sure he could spot the large man from a mile away.

Nothing.

"I don't see them," Art replied. "But there's no sense in taking chances."

He pointed at a large tour group getting ready to enter the chapel. "Let's tag along and try to blend in," he said. "Maybe we won't stand out quite as much if we're part of a group."

They made their way to the back of the tour group and patiently stood in line to enter the chapel.

The tour group entered the chapel by way of a small door on the side of the massive building. A volunteer near the entrance handed out guide maps as the group filed into the church. Art opened his map and immediately tried to identify the location of Henry VI's tomb.

"Wow," Camille said.

Art looked up from the guide map. They were standing in the nave, the central section of the chapel—the area where people would sit for services. Camille was staring up at the ceiling high above their heads. It was an incredible sight. The ceiling was a spider web of intricately carved stonework. Each stone column rising from the nave floor separated and branched off into multiple lines that crisscrossed the ceiling. At the intersections of the lines were innumerable coats of arms and other odd symbols carved into the stone. It was almost overwhelming.

Art turned toward the huge window at the far end of the nave. He counted five rows of ornately decorated stained-glass windows with at least fifteen separate windows per row. The detail in each window was remarkable.

Art could not help but admire the craftsmanship and talent that it had taken to build the chapel. It was not simply a building—it was a massive work of art that had taken more than fifty years to construct. The architecture, the sculptures, the stonework, the stained glass. All of it was extraordinary. But it also posed a significant problem for Camille and Art on their quest to solve the next line in the riddle: *Whence youth now sleeps three saints reside, ye second signs held by her side.*

"This place is *filled* with signs and symbols," Art said. "There are images of saints everywhere."

"Not going to be easy, is it?" Camille said.

The tour group had moved down the center of the chapel toward the west side of the church. Art motioned for Camille to follow him over to one of the large columns in the side aisle. The two weren't completely hidden—but they were no longer standing exposed to everyone in the chapel. Camille glanced down the side aisle and then back out into the center of the church for any sign of her father or his large companion. Everything was clear.

Although the temperature inside the cathedral was cool, Camille noticed that Art was sweating. She glanced down at his arm. It was now covered by a long-sleeved shirt, but she could tell by the way he held it at his side that he was in terrible pain.

Art caught her staring at him.

"It's okay," he said. "Let's just find the three saints and get out of here."

Art glanced at the guide map of the chapel. "According to the map, Henry VI's grave is located at the far end of the aisle right next to us."

Camille peeked around the stone column. The aisle was dimly lit and crowded with tourists, but—again—there was no sign of her father or the thief.

"Looks clear," she said.

Camille and Art made their way slowly down the aisle. Despite the large crowd of tourists in the chapel, it was quiet —only the shuffling of feet and faint whispers broke the silence.

"There," Art said. He was pointing at a thick slab of gray stone to their left. A black iron railing ran around the top of the stone. They made their way over to the iron railing. On top of the gray stone slab was another stone slab —deep black in color with the words "HENRY VI" inlaid in brass.

Camille stared at the words on the grave. Before this morning she had never even heard of King Henry VI. But in just the past three hours, she had been to the chapel where his life had ended and now stood at the spot where he had been buried. And despite everything that was going on around her, it was not lost on Camille that Henry VI was not simply some character in a story or the answer to a riddle on an hourglass. He had been a real person. She reminded herself not to forget that.

CHAPTER 40

Art stepped back from the tomb and looked around.

There was no hint of three saints or anything that could reasonably be construed as having anything to do with one saint, let alone three. There was nothing carved or painted on the tomb that appeared to be related to the riddle — just an engraved medallion and the king's name. There was nothing in the stained-glass window behind them. There was nothing in the stone carvings in the area around the tomb. There was nothing engraved, carved, or inscribed on the floor or the ceiling.

Nothing.

"I don't see anything," Camille said. "Maybe we're in the wrong place?"

Art shook his head. "No," he replied. "It's here — somewhere."

* * *

Broderick Tinsley stood on the walkway at the east end of the lower ward. St George's Chapel rose majestically to his right. He closed his eyes and took a deep breath.

"Why did you stop?" demanded Miles Davenport. "We don't have time for this."

"The chapel is around five hundred years old," said Broderick. "It's filled with hundreds of intricately detailed stained-glass windows."

"You're wasting time," said Davenport.

Broderick ignored him. His eyes remained closed. "There are," he continued, "literally tens of thousands of stone carvings and inscriptions inside the chapel. Some of them are a hundred feet or more above the floor."

Davenport grabbed Broderick by the arm. "Then we need to get into the chapel," he said. "Now!"

Broderick opened his eyes and stared at Davenport. "We are searching for a needle in a haystack, and I need time to sort out the next clue."

Davenport let go of Broderick's arm. "So what's your plan?" he asked.

Broderick had spent almost all of his time trying to decipher the first line of the riddle from the hourglass. He knew that the second clue would be at St George's Chapel —the location of Henry VI's tomb—but not much more. He needed a week—perhaps more—of intense research and thought. He needed to spend time roaming through the chapel and exploring its history.

But he didn't have time.

So what was his plan?

There was only one way to handle this.

"We get some help," he said.

Art closed his eyes and repeated the second line of the riddle: "Whence youth now sleeps three saints reside, ye second signs held by her side." He opened his eyes.

"Okay," Art said. "So what do we know? No guessing, just facts."

"Well, we know three saints have something to do with it," said Camille.

Camille's observation was obvious but absolutely correct.

"And whatever we're looking for has to be pretty old," said Art. "At least as old as the hourglass. And the riddle says 'her side,' so we know there's a woman involved."

"Or it could be a girl," Camille said. "You never know."

Art nodded. Camille was right. No guessing.

"And," said Art, "whatever the next sign is, it's *next* to her. Anything else?"

"The riddle actually says the sign is *held* by her side," Camille replied. "Maybe she's holding the sign?"

"Good point," Art said. "So here's what we know: The answer to the riddle has to involve three saints. It has to be at least as old—maybe older—than the hourglass. There's a woman or girl involved, and she has something next to her—she might even be holding it."

Art looked around the chapel. It was filled with thousands of engravings, carvings, stained glass, and inscriptions. It would take a lifetime to sort through them all.

"So what next?" Camille asked.

"We get some help," replied Art.

CHAPTER 41

1:54 p.m.
Thursday, August 14
St George's Chapel
Windsor, England

Camille followed Art down the aisle to the entrance to the chapel. Ahead of them stood a tall, bald man in a red robe speaking to a group of tourists. Camille and Art stopped just short of the small gathering.

"What are we doing?" whispered Camille.

"Waiting," replied Art. "For help."

"And, once again," the man said to the group standing in front of him, "I want to thank you for visiting the College of St George and this magnificent chapel. I hope you've enjoyed your visit."

Camille and Art stood back and watched as several members of the tour group surrounded the man in the red robe and shook his hand. Finally, when it appeared that the thank-yous had tapered to an end, Art approached the man.

"Excuse me," Art said. "Are you a tour guide?"

The man smiled. "I conduct tours," he replied politely,

"but technically I'm a steward—a member of the Guild of Stewards of the College of St George."

"I'm sorry," said Art. "I didn't mean to call you a tour guide."

"Not a problem whatsoever," the man said. "My name is Nigel Alvey. How may I be of service?"

"My friend and I need help finding something in the chapel," replied Art. "We're on sort of a scavenger hunt, and we've hit a complete dead end."

The steward's eyes lit up. "A scavenger hunt!" he said. "I must say, that's an excellent way to learn about the chapel! Well, let's see if I can help solve this little mystery."

"This is all we know," Art said. He rattled off the clues from the riddle: three saints, old, a woman or a girl, a sign by her side.

"Hmmm," the steward said. "That's all quite mysterious and intriguing, but I'm afraid nothing immediately jumps to mind. There are certainly lots of images of saints within the chapel, but I'm afraid I can't think of anything that matches everything on your list."

The disappointment was evident on Art's face. "Well," he said, "thank you for trying . . ."

"Trying?" said the steward. "Trying? Do or do not. There is no try—and I'm not done yet."

"Wait a second," interjected Camille. "Did you just quote Yoda?"

"Aye," replied the steward. "And there's a lot more

where that came from. Now, let's find this . . . well . . . what-ever it is."

"I like this guy," Camille whispered to Art.

Broderick made his way across the broad lawn of the lower ward, followed close behind by Miles Davenport. They passed the entrance to St George's Chapel and continued walking.

"Exactly where are we headed?" demanded Davenport.

"The horseshoe," said Broderick.

"The horseshoe?" asked Davenport. "You better know what you're doing, or I swear I'll pitch you from the top of that chapel."

Broderick had little doubt that Davenport would do exactly as he promised.

Just past the west end of the chapel, they walked through a stone archway and into a small courtyard. To their left was a long two-story building in the shape of a semicircle. It was constructed of deep red brick and thick wooden timbers.

"This is the Horseshoe Cloister," Broderick explained as he continued straight across the courtyard toward a tall building constructed of stone with a slate roof. Broderick made his way over to an arched red door. A small brass plaque next to the door read:

VICARS' HALL UNDERCROFT

ST GEORGE'S CHAPEL ARCHIVES AND CHAPTER LIBRARY

"We don't have time to read a bunch of books," said Davenport.

Broderick opened the door. "I'm not here to read."

CHAPTER 42

Volunteers dressed in the traditional red robes of the Guild of Stewards had greeted visitors to St George's Chapel for generations. Every day, seven guild members—and only seven members—roamed the aisles, nave, and quire of the chapel ready to answer questions or simply lend a hand. Occasionally a steward might have sought the assistance of a more experienced volunteer, many of whom had served the College of St George for decades. It remained, however, a rare occasion to find two or more stewards gathered together on the floor of the chapel for any significant length of time. There was far too much to do and far too many visitors to assist. To find all seven stewards gathered together? It simply did not happen.

Until today.

The stewards—four men and three women draped in red—stood around Art and Camille.

"I'm telling you," insisted a short, round man. "It's referring to St. Edward the Confessor and St. George."

177

"Come now, Darby," said a tall, thin woman. "The young man said three saints, not two."

"And last time I checked," said an ancient-looking man with a tall, thin face, "neither Edward nor George were of the female persuasion."

Darby blushed, his face turning the color of his robe. The tall, thin woman patted him on the back. "At least they're saints," she said. "You got that much right."

Darby pulled back his plump shoulders and stood as straight as he could. "Nothing ventured, nothing gained!" he exclaimed.

"That's the spirit!" exclaimed another steward. "Now let's solve this mystery for our young guests."

The stewards continued to debate among themselves exactly what the clues could have meant. Camille glanced over at Art. The long-sleeved shirt, bought back at the station, covered up his arm and he was doing his best not to let on how bad it was hurting, but she could tell. She knew that he needed to get to a doctor soon.

"Excuse me," a deep voice said.

The stewards stopped speaking immediately. Camille turned to find a short, white-haired man standing in the nave just a few feet away. He was wearing a black robe with a red shirt and white clerical collar. He had a stern look on his face.

"It's the dean," the steward named Darby whispered to Camille.

"The dean?" Camille asked.

"Aye," whispered Darby. "He's the head of the College of St George. And because St George is a Royal Peculiar, he was appointed by the queen herself."

"Royal Peculiar?" whispered Camille. That seemed like a strange name for a church.

"Aye," replied Darby. "There are certain churches in England that fall directly under the queen's authority. They're called Royal Peculiars."

"Nice lady, the queen," said Camille. "I met her earlier this year."

Darby shot a sideways glance at Camille. "Codswallop," he whispered.

"And what is the occasion for this impromptu meeting of the guild?" asked the dean.

"Just helping a couple of visitors," replied Nigel Alvey. He gestured at Camille and Art.

The dean looked at Camille. "I am the Right Reverend Joseph Bernard. And with whom do I have the pleasure of speaking?" he asked.

"Camille Sullivan," she replied. "And this is my friend Art—Art Hamilton."

"Art and Camille!" Darby exclaimed. "The young people who stopped that art theft in the States?"

"Yes," replied Camille, who was obviously excited at being recognized.

"Blimey," said Darby. "So you *did* meet the queen?"

"I did," replied Camille.

Another round of animated discussion commenced among the stewards.

"Ahem," the deep voice interrupted once more.

Once again the stewards fell silent.

"And what brings the two of you to St George's Chapel?" asked the dean.

"They're on a scavenger hunt," interjected Nigel Alvey. He explained the clues to the dean.

The tall, thin woman spoke up. "So far we've had no luck in solving the clues," she said. "And we know the chapel about as well as anyone."

The stewards all nodded in agreement.

"True," the dean said. "But what you are looking for is not in the chapel."

CHAPTER 43

1:59 p.m.
Thursday, August 14
Vicars' Hall Undercroft, St George's Chapel Archives and Chapter Library
Windsor, England

The clerk at the information desk, a young woman by the name of Shruti, looked up at Broderick and Davenport.

"May I speak with Dr. Elizabeth Cookson, please?" Broderick said.

"Do you have an appointment?" the clerk asked politely.

"No," Broderick replied.

"I'm afraid that you must have an appointment to see Dr. Cookson," the clerk said. "She's terribly busy."

"I understand," Broderick replied. He scribbled his name on a piece of paper and handed it to the clerk. "Would you mind letting Dr. Cookson know I am here and that I need her assistance? I promise it won't take long."

The clerk hesitated.

"Just ask," said Broderick. "Please?"

The clerk nodded and headed toward the rear of the library.

* * *

Under normal circumstances Shruti would have firmly, but politely, informed an unexpected visitor that an appointment was absolutely necessary. She would not even have considered troubling Dr. Cookson with a request like this. And there were certainly good reasons for sticking with her normal protocol. But the large man with the mustache absolutely creeped her out. The quicker he left the library, the better. And there was another very good reason why she agreed to the other man's request — the name on the piece of paper in her hand.

Shruti knocked lightly on Dr. Cookson's door.

"Come in," a woman's voice called from within the room.

Shruti opened the door and made her way over to the large desk in the middle of the room. The desk was piled high with books and papers. Dr. Elizabeth Cookson looked up at Shruti over a pair of reading glasses.

"Yes, Shruti?" she asked.

"Someone . . . is here to see you."

Dr. Cookson glanced at the calendar on her desk. There were no appointments scheduled.

"Ask them to make an appointment," she replied. "I'm up to my eyeballs in research."

Shruti placed the piece of paper on the desk in front of Dr. Cookson. "He asked me to tell you he was here and needed your assistance. He said it wouldn't take much of your time."

Dr. Elizabeth Cookson picked up the piece of paper and read the name.

A middle-aged woman with long black hair interspersed with streaks of white made her way to the receptionist's desk. She wore a loose-fitting blouse, a tie-dyed wrap skirt, and sandals. A pair of reading glasses hung from a long chain around her neck.

She extended her hand to Broderick. "Professor Tinsley?" she said.

Broderick nodded.

"I'm Dr. Elizabeth Cookson, head archivist and chapter librarian for St George's Chapel," she continued. "But please call me Beth. It's an honor to have you with us this afternoon. I've followed your work for years. Quite impressive and exciting — particularly that situation with the excavation in Leeds that you described in your TED Talk. I can't believe you managed to escape that with your life."

"Thank you," said Broderick. "And I do apologize for barging in without an appointment."

Broderick then gestured at Miles Davenport. "And this is Fred, my secretary."

Davenport's mustache twitched ever so slightly. "Hello," he grunted.

"And how might I be of service?" asked Dr. Cookson.

"I've reached a bit of an impasse in some research," said

Broderick. "I was wondering if you might be able to assist on a minor detail?"

Dr. Cookson's eyes went wide. The chance to assist in research for one of the most important historians in England was irresistible.

"Why, of course," she gushed.

She motioned for Broderick to follow her. "Please," she said, "let's have some tea in my office while we discuss this."

Broderick looked at Davenport. "Fred," he said, "why don't you wait in the reception area. We won't be long. You can check my messages while you're waiting."

Davenport glared at Broderick. "Aye," he finally said. "I'll be here . . . waiting on you."

CHAPTER 44

2:02 p.m.
Thursday, August 14
St George's Chapel
Windsor, England

"What do you mean it's not in the chapel?" asked Art.

The dean looked at the stewards. "The Catherine Room," he said.

"Of course!" exclaimed Nigel Alvey.

"Scones and tea!" said Darby. "How could we have missed that?"

"Because you were focused on the chapel itself," the dean replied. "But the cloisters are an essential part of the College of St George."

"The cloisters?" asked Camille. "What are cloisters?"

The dean gestured toward the interior of the chapel. "This may be the house of the Lord," he said, "but it has been served for centuries by men and women who have dedicated their lives to caring for it — many of whom have lived within the castle walls. The cloisters are where they reside."

Reside. Art wanted to kick himself. That was one word he and Camille had completely overlooked in the riddle: "Whence youth now sleeps three saints *reside.*"

"And the Catherine Room?" asked Art. "Why do you think that's what we're looking for?"

"Follow me," the dean said as he headed across the nave to the north side of the church.

All seven stewards, Art, and Camille started to follow.

The dean stopped. He turned and looked at the group following him. "Let me correct myself," he said. "Art, Camille, and Nigel—follow me. The rest of you, try to find someone else to assist."

There was a groan of disappointment from the six remaining stewards.

"Just when it was getting good," complained Darby as he headed back toward the entrance.

The dean, Camille, Art, and Nigel made their way down the nave of the chapel and out the large doors at the western end of the church. A light mist had started to fall.

The dean continued down the stairs to the courtyard below. To their right was a stone archway. The dean led them through the archway and into another, much larger courtyard. On the north side of the courtyard was a row of ancient brick and timber homes. The houses seemed to have been piled one on top of another.

"This is the Horseshoe Cloister," explained Nigel Alvey. "The deans and canons of the College of St George have lived here for centuries."

He looked down at Camille. "This is quite a privilege," he said. "Very few visitors are allowed back here."

Camille nodded. She turned and looked back at the imposing façade of St George's Chapel, which formed one side of the courtyard. Low clouds clung to the top of the chapel.

The dean continued across the courtyard and stopped in front of a wooden doorway at one of the brick and timber buildings. A small enamel sign next to the door identified it as NO. 2.

The dean unlocked the door and held it open as Camille, Art, and Nigel entered. The room was empty. Following them and pulling the door shut, the dean relocked it and then proceeded across the room to a small, narrow stairway.

"Be careful," the dean warned as he ascended the stairs. "There are no lights in the stairway, and it can be quite dark."

Camille ran her hand along the wall as she started up the stairs. It was incredible that a building more than six hundred years old was still used by the chapel.

"This building," the dean said as he made his way up the stairs, "was originally constructed in the fourteenth century. During a renovation of the cloisters back in 1965, the construction workers discovered something quite unusual."

The dean reached a small landing, turned left, and continued up the stairs. By this point, it was far too dark to see where they were going. Camille kept her hand on the wall to her right as she navigated the cramped and uneven staircase. Finally the dean reached the top of the stairway and opened a small wooden door. The gray light of the overcast day reflected through the windows of the room and illu-minated the narrow stairway. The light—dim as it was—temporarily blinded her, and Camille threw up her hands to cover her eyes.

"Sorry about that," said the dean. "I should have warned you."

Camille, Art, and Nigel continued up the last few stairs and stepped into a large timber-framed room. Nigel closed the door behind them. The dean was standing in the middle of the room facing them.

"Welcome to the Catherine Room," said the dean. "The home of the three saints."

CHAPTER 45

Dr. Elizabeth Cookson poured a cup of tea for her guest and then settled into a well-worn armchair.

"Now," she said, "how may I be of service to you?"

"We are seeking three saints," said Broderick.

"Three saints?" asked Dr. Cookson. "I'm not sure I understand."

Broderick pulled a pad of paper from his jacket and scribbled down the second line from the hourglass: "Whence youth now sleeps three saints reside, ye second signs held by her side."

He handed the pad to Dr. Cookson. "I'm afraid I don't have time for a more detailed explanation," he said. "I just need to know if this means anything to you."

Dr. Cookson put on her reading glasses and read the words on the pad.

She glanced over the top of her glasses at Broderick. "Research?" she asked.

189

"Research," Broderick replied.

Dr. Cookson smiled. "I don't know what this is all about," she said, "but I believe I know where you can find your three saints."

2:07 p.m.
Thursday, August 14
Catherine Room, the Cloisters
Windsor, England

The ancient floorboards creaked as they stepped into the room. Dark wooden timbers crisscrossed on the ceiling and the walls. The space between the timbers was filled with whitewashed wattle and daub. High on the walls, and just below the ceiling, was a series of murals, the colors muted with age.

"The murals," said the dean, "were discovered during the renovation of the cloisters in the 1960s. We were putting in a fire suppression system and discovered that a false ceiling had been added to the room centuries ago. The murals were hidden behind the ceiling."

"Wow!" exclaimed Art. There were large gaps in the murals where the plaster on which the murals had been painted had fallen off. Still—after more than five hundred years—the effect was incredible. Art could only imagine what the room would have looked like at the time the murals were painted. It would have been spectacular—the colors far brighter, the details crisper. He wondered if his father had ever heard about or visited the Catherine Room.

The dean pointed to the mural on the wall directly opposite the stairway. It was an image of a man holding what appeared to be a spear and a book. To his right was a lamb.

"That is St. John the Baptist," he said. "We believe it was painted around 1486—give or take a few years."

One saint, Art noted. *Two to go.*

The dean turned to an image of a male figure on the wall to his left. "St. George," he said. "The patron saint of the college."

Two saints.

Finally, the dean turned to his right. On the wall were images of two women. One woman stood in front of a tree filled with a round red fruit. The other woman stood holding a wheel with images of more wheels by her side.

"Two women?" asked Camille. "I thought we were looking for just one."

"No," the dean replied. "You are looking for three saints—and only one of the women is a saint. Do you see the woman with the fruit tree?"

Camille edged closer to the wall and looked up at the mural. "Yes," she said. "Are those apples?"

"Actually," replied the dean, "they're pomegranates.

They are the symbol of Catherine of Aragon, Henry VIII's first wife."

"And the other lady?" she asked.

"Another Catherine," the dean replied. "Catherine of Alexandria—also known as St. Catherine of the Wheel."

This is it, Art thought.

Whence youth now sleeps three saints reside, ye second signs held by her side.

Three saints.

One woman.

And a sign.

Art looked at Camille. "Wheels," he said.

Camille pulled out her phone and snapped a picture.

They now had two signs: wheels and the word *sator*. The signs didn't make any sense yet, but they could work on putting the pieces together during the train ride back to London. The next and last step: a trip to Westminster Abbey.

The sound of footsteps and a door shutting in the room below interrupted Art's train of thought.

"Sounds like the Catherine Room is a popular destination today," said Nigel. He seemed genuinely surprised. "Usually the only people who visit are academics. It's not like you can just wander in here."

It took a moment for Nigel's words to register with Art.

A trip to the Catherine Room was not one of the usual tourist destinations at Windsor Castle. In fact, Art had never even heard of the Catherine Room until this afternoon, even though he had been to Windsor on innumerable occasions. He imagined that the only people who visited the room had a specific reason to do so—like they did.

Like Professor Broderick Tinsley did.

Like the large man—the thief—did.

Art's arm immediately started to ache.

CHAPTER 46

2:11 p.m.
Thursday, August 14
Catherine Room, the Cloisters
Windsor, England

Art glanced anxiously around the room. They needed to find a way out—and quick. If Broderick was in the room below, then he probably wasn't alone. But the Catherine Room offered no exit other than the way they had entered. There were three leaded windows on the wall to the right, but they did not appear as if they had been opened for centuries. A narrow brick fireplace set into the wall on the far side of the room offered no better option.

He caught Camille's attention. It was clear that she was thinking the same thing.

We have to go, he mouthed silently. *Now.*

Camille tapped the dean on his arm. "Sir," she said, "thanks for all your help, but we have a train to catch. My mom will kill us if we're not home on time."

The dean smiled. "Of course, of course," he replied. "Let's get you on your way, shall we?"

The dean turned to Nigel Alvey. "If you don't mind,

would you escort our guests to the exit? I'll stay behind and greet our next group of visitors."

Nigel Alvey bowed. "My pleasure," he said.

Camille and Art thanked the dean for his assistance and followed Nigel to the top of the stairway.

"What are we going to do?" whispered Camille.

"I don't know," said Art.

As they reached the door, they could hear the murmur of voices from below. One voice stood out loud and clear. It was the thief.

Art's arm throbbed with pain.

We're trapped, he realized.

Broderick was surprised that he had never heard of the Catherine Room. Based on Dr. Cookson's description, however, it appeared to be exactly what they were looking for. It now seemed so obvious. The clue seemed so simple.

Broderick paused.

But that's stupid, he told himself. *There is nothing simple about this.*

The clue he was following was four hundred years old. When the clue had been engraved onto the hourglass, there were no guidebooks, tour guides, archivists, or historians to consult. There was no Internet. There were probably only a handful of people in England who even knew about the

Catherine Room. The cloisters were the private quarters of the deans and canons of St George's Chapel, located within the thick stone walls of Windsor Castle. The solution—whatever it may turn out to be—would have been exceptionally well-hidden.

No, there is nothing simple about this clue.

Dr. Cookson was describing the history of the cloisters as they started up the stairs to the Catherine Room. Dr. Cookson led the way, followed by Broderick and, finally, Miles Davenport.

As they ascended the dark stairway, Davenport grabbed Broderick by the back of his neck and pulled him close.

"Call me your secretary again," Davenport growled, "and I'll rip your arm off."

Broderick didn't respond. He knew that Davenport was quite capable of doing just that—and that he would probably enjoy it.

"That's unusual," said Dr. Cookson. "It sounds as if someone is already in the Catherine Room."

The hair on the back of Broderick's neck went up immediately.

He had a sinking feeling that he knew who was in the room at the top of the stairs.

"I have to throw up," Camille announced suddenly.

Nigel Alvey looked at her in alarm. Cleaning up vomit

was not on his list of approved volunteer activities. And he had just had his robe dry-cleaned.

"As soon as the stairs are clear, we'll head down to the courtyard," he said. "Can you wait that long?"

Camille covered her mouth with her hand and shook her head.

"Down! Now!" said Nigel as he threw open the door and started down the narrow staircase. Crowded or not, he was intent on clearing a path for his young visitor.

The sudden and unexpected flood of light into the narrow staircase blinded Dr. Cookson. She threw her hands up in an effort to block the brightness. In doing so, she temporarily lost her balance and fell back into Professor Tinsley, who grabbed her and held on for dear life. Broderick looked over her shoulder to the room above to see what had happened. Out of the brightness emerged a large red object. It was descending on them quickly.

Nigel Alvey had only a moment to consider what was unfolding. His red robe flapped madly as he made his way down the narrow stairway. The woman in front of him — he realized almost immediately that it was Dr. Cookson, the archivist — had fallen backwards. Nigel leaned forward to grab her.

* * *

Camille and Art ducked into the stairwell directly behind the steward. His large red robe provided some cover in the narrow passage.

Art grabbed the door leading into the Catherine Room and pulled it shut.

The staircase was — once again — completely dark.

Art stepped down into the darkness. It was impossible to see where he was going. He reached out with his left hand. It struck something — someone.

Nigel Alvey was standing on the stairs, his hand extended toward Dr. Cookson, when the stairwell suddenly went dark. The unexpected loss of light was disorienting, and he reached out to the wall to steady himself.

That was close, Nigel thought.

And then suddenly he felt something — someone — strike him in the back.

Nigel fell forward into the darkness.

"I've got you," Broderick said to Dr. Cookson just before the stairway suddenly went dark once more.

And he did have her. And for a brief moment, everything seemed fine.

"Well, that was close," Dr. Cookson said with a nervous laugh.

And that's when the full weight of Nigel Alvey, Steward of the College of St George, came crashing down upon her.

For a moment—a very brief moment—Broderick held his own.

Miles Davenport stood on the landing in the middle of the stairway. Their ascent up the stairs had come to a sudden stop, but it was impossible in the darkness to see what was happening. Davenport—his patience at an end—whipped out his cell phone and activated the flashlight. Above him, Davenport could just make out Broderick Tinsley leaning precariously backwards.

"What the dickens is going on?" Davenport exclaimed.

Broderick glanced back over his shoulder at Davenport. "Help," he wheezed as he collapsed backwards.

Instinctively Davenport reached out to grab Broderick. Broderick's back hit him flush in the chest and drove him backwards into the wall of the landing. Davenport's cell phone flew out of his grasp and tumbled down the staircase. Once more he found himself in darkness. Almost immediately Davenport realized that it was much more than Broderick that he was now holding. Davenport was trapped, his back pinned firmly against the wall by the bodies piled up in front of him.

* * *

Camille heard the bodies tumbling in the darkness below. She heard Broderick exclaim that someone's foot was in his ear.

Oh no! she thought.

She had not meant for this to happen. She had simply hoped to rush past them in the darkness.

Suddenly a hand grabbed her and started dragging her down the stairs.

"Come on," Art whispered. "We've got to get out of here."

Pushing her back up against the stairway wall, Camille held tightly to Art's hand as they made their way down the stairs. As they reached the landing in the middle of the stairway, they could make out Nigel Alvey lying on top of several people scrunched against the back wall of the landing. His red robe had flown up over his head and now lay over the pile of bodies. An effort was under way to untangle the mass of arms, legs, and torsos.

Camille heard Broderick ask if everyone was okay.

His question elicited a chorus of comments and curse words — but everyone appeared to be fine, if a bit perturbed.

The Right Reverend Joseph Bernard flung open the door at the top of the stairs. Light once again flooded the stairway.

"My word!" the dean exclaimed. "Is everyone okay?"

The dean's question elicited yet another chorus of comments and curse words.

Miles Davenport was seeing red.

Literally.

A thick red robe covered his face, and both of his arms were pinned tight against his body by the weight on top of him. He pushed forward on the pile with his shoulders and, with a jerk, pulled his right arm free. Davenport snatched the red cloth from his face. It was a robe, he quickly discovered, attached to a man lying on top of the jumble of bodies.

Davenport glanced up at the top of the stairs. A distinguished-looking gentleman in a black robe and red shirt was standing there, a look of concern on his face.

And that's when he heard it—the sound of footsteps heading down the stairs. Davenport tried to look to his left, but his view was blocked by a black sneaker attached to a leg. He grabbed the shoe and twisted it so that he could see down the stairs.

"Ow!" exclaimed Broderick. "That's my foot!"

Davenport gave Broderick's foot another twist for good measure.

"Ow!" Broderick exclaimed again.

With the foot out of the way, Davenport had a clear view of the stairway below.

Art reached the bottom of the stairs first.

"C'mon," he urged Camille.

Art glanced back up the stairway as Camille bounded out the door and into the courtyard.

The large man with the mustache was staring back at him.

CHAPTER 47

It took another two minutes to sort out the pile, get everyone back to their feet, and confirm that no one had been injured.

Nigel Alvey apologized profusely for knocking everyone down. He seemed genuinely embarrassed by the whole episode.

"I'm afraid it was a bit of a medical emergency," he started to explain to Dr. Cookson. "You see, the young—"

"Don't worry yourself," interrupted Broderick. "These things happen. A bit of a shock, but no worse for the wear. Sorry to have to run, but we're in a bit of a hurry. I hope you understand."

"Well, of course," said the steward. "I just wanted to—"

"I'll not hear of it," interrupted Broderick once more. "An accident—nothing more. No need for apologies."

Broderick grabbed the steward's hand, shook it profusely, thanked him for his concern, and then hurried Dr.

Cookson and Davenport up the stairway and into the Catherine Room.

Art and Camille sprinted across the courtyard and ducked behind a row of hedges near the chapel.

"He . . . saw . . . me," Art panted as he tried to catch his breath.

"Who?" asked Camille. "My dad?"

"No," replied Art. "The big guy—the thief."

Uh-oh, Camille thought.

"Do you think he recognized you?" she asked.

"I don't know," said Art. "Maybe . . . possibly." He was still wearing the cap and the shirt he had purchased at the train station, but he wondered if it was enough of a disguise.

Art took a deep breath. The situation was getting more perilous and uncertain by the minute. The pain in his arm was a sharp reminder of what the man with Camille's father was capable of doing. While Camille and Art had located the first two signs from the poem, they still had no idea what they meant. The answer to the third part of the riddle —*O'er ye heavens youth was crowned, ye signs reveal what time hath bound*—waited for them unsolved at Westminster Abbey. And now an overgrown psychopath may have figured out that they were chasing the same treasure.

The sound of footsteps clomping across the stone

pavers in the courtyard cut off any further discussion. Art and Camille peeked around the hedge. The steward was making his way across the courtyard. He had a worried look on his face.

"Nigel's heading this way," said Camille. "We need to get out of here."

Art shook his head. "We can't," he replied. "At least not yet. What if Nigel panics and starts searching for us? He could alert the guards and the other stewards. That could lead to all sorts of questions."

Art peeked around the corner of the hedge once more to make sure Nigel was alone.

He turned back to Camille. "We don't need those questions."

Art stood and waved at the steward.

Camille watched as Nigel Alvey looked frantically around the courtyard. Art waved once more to get the steward's attention. She could see the relief on his face when he spotted them. Nigel made his way quickly across the courtyard, where he found them behind the hedge.

"Are you okay?" he asked Camille.

"Yes," she replied. "I'm sorry about that. Oyster stew for lunch. I hope no one was hurt."

"Everyone's fine," replied the steward. "Don't worry yourself a bit."

"Thanks for all the help," said Art. "But we really need to catch the train back to London."

"Actually," Camille interjected, "I did have one question before we go."

"We really need to get going," Art said.

Camille glanced at Art. "One question," she said. The tone in her voice foreclosed any further objection from Art.

Camille then turned back to Nigel. "One of the other stewards told me that St George's is a Royal Peculiar."

"Aye," the steward replied.

"A royal what?" Art asked.

"I'll explain later," Camille said to Art. She liked the idea that she actually knew something about history that Art did not—even though she had only learned about it less than an hour ago.

She turned back to the steward. "Are there other Royal Peculiars?" Camille asked.

"Several," Nigel replied.

"The Tower of London and Westminster Abbey?" Camille asked. "Are they Royal Peculiars?"

The steward seemed surprised. "As a matter of fact," he replied, "they are."

Camille nodded and glanced at Art. The confused look on his face was so worth it.

* * *

Broderick stood in front of the mural of St. Catherine.

Dr. Cookson had excused herself and was now speaking with the dean on the far side of the room.

"A wheel?" asked Davenport.

"Wheels," Broderick replied.

There was a brief moment of silence as both men stared at the mural.

"You know what all of this means, don't you?" Davenport finally said.

Broderick nodded. He did know. He'd known as soon as he'd seen the image of St. Catherine. All the pieces now fit together. The sign from Wakefield Tower. The wheels. Everything.

He knew exactly what to look for at Westminster Abbey—and exactly where he would find it.

Davenport didn't need to be a great detective to know they were being followed by—or perhaps had been unknowingly following—the boy. But the boy was not alone. A girl with red hair was with the boy. And while Davenport had seen only the back of the young girl's head from the stairs, he had recognized her immediately. It was the same girl that he had photographed in Washington, DC. It was Tinsley's daughter.

Davenport considered his options. The kids were clearly

a factor that could not be ignored. He had encountered the boy at the Tower of London. He could only assume that the girl had been there as well. And now it appeared that the two of them had actually uncovered the second clue. The girl and the boy were now officially part of the equation. He cursed himself for not taking care of the boy when he'd had a chance. Davenport vowed that he would not hesitate the next time.

The timeline, it seemed, had changed once again.

Fortunately, he had already made arrangements.

Davenport took out his phone and dialed.

"Hello?" a man answered. Davenport could hear the nervousness in the man's voice.

Good. The man needed to be nervous.

"We're coming tonight," Davenport said.

"Tonight?" the voice replied. "But I can't . . . My wife has made plans to . . ."

"Tonight," Davenport repeated. "Open by six o'clock —right after Evensong. Understood?"

There was a pause on the line.

"Understood," the voice finally replied. "It will be open."

Davenport hung up the phone. Across the room Broderick and Dr. Cookson continued to discuss the mural.

Only Westminster Abbey remained.

CHAPTER 48

3:15 p.m.
Thursday, August 14
Windsor & Eton Central Railway Station
Windsor, England

Art and Camille found seats in the rear car of the train back to London.

"We need to get to Westminster Abbey," Art said.

Art was right. They did need to get to Westminster Abbey. But Camille knew that there was a more immediate concern. Art wasn't complaining about the pain in his arm, but Camille could see it in his face every time he moved or shifted in his seat.

"We need to do something about your arm," she said.

Art shrugged. "It'll be okay."

"Have you tried Googling the terms 'sower' and 'wheels' on your phone?" he asked, a clear effort to change the subject.

"Yes," Camille replied. "Tons of results—nothing good."

Art nodded and closed his eyes. He looked exhausted.

Camille sat back and stared out the window at the countryside rushing past. Dark rain clouds now sat low in the sky. In the distance she could see a thick column of rain making its way over a treeless hill.

Camille pulled out her phone and checked for messages. Nothing. She had told her mom they would be back at the hotel by five o'clock, and they still had plenty of time to make it. But they needed to go to Westminster Abbey. They needed to try to solve the final line of the riddle. They needed to try to save her father.

Camille glanced over at Art.

She knew what she had to do.

Camille texted her mom.

She then closed her eyes and tried to get a little rest, but her mind would not stop racing.

Sator.

The clue from the Tower of London.

It was, they had realized, a Latin term that meant "sower" — someone who spreads seeds in a field. That made sense. The image in the stained-glass windows at Wakefield Tower was a man spreading seeds.

But the second sign had been just a mural of a bunch of wheels.

No words.

No Latin.

Camille opened her eyes and sat upright.

She pulled out her phone and Googled the phrase "Latin word for wheel."

According to the first website she found, the Latin word for "wheel" was *rota*.

Rota?

Another dead end.

And then Camille remembered: The sign wasn't a wheel —it was *wheels*. And the second line of the riddle spoke of *signs* —plural also.

Camille scrolled down the page on her phone until she found a small chart with the various forms of the word *rota* in Latin.

Jeez, she thought, *could Latin be any more complicated?*

She found the plural version of the word in the chart.

She stared at the word. There was something oddly familiar about it.

And then a revelation hit her.

Holy cow!

"Art!" she exclaimed.

CHAPTER 49

"Art!"

He ignored the noise. Sleep dulled the pain in his arm.

"Art!"

"Art!"

The noise persisted. He kept his eyes closed.

"Art!"

"Art!"

It was clear she wasn't going to shut up.

"Yes?" Art asked. He opened his eyes. Camille was pointing at her phone.

"Do you know what the Latin word for 'wheels' is?"

There was a broad grin on Camille's face.

"No," he replied. "I don't."

Camille handed Art her phone and pointed at the screen. "There," she said.

Art looked down at the word: *rotas.*

He sat upright in his seat.

"I've seen this word," he said excitedly. "I saw it at the Tower, but it was . . . different."

He was now wide-awake. His mind rushed to process the information. Where had he seen the word?

"You did see it!" Camille said. "It's *sator* spelled backwards! The Latin word for 'wheels' is *sator* spelled backwards!"

"Wakefield Tower!" exclaimed Art. "It was the word in the window at Wakefield Tower, but the letters were backwards. That can't be a coincidence."

Before Camille could respond, her phone rang. It was her mother. In all of the excitement, Camille had forgotten about the text message she had sent her.

Camille answered the call. "Hey, Mom," she said.

She paused and listened.

"Yes, ma'am," she replied.

A longer pause.

"Yes, ma'am," she replied again. "We'll meet you there."

Camille ended the call.

"What was that all about?" asked Art.

"Change of plans," said Camille.

"Change of plans?" asked Art. "Aren't we going to Westminster Abbey?"

"No," Camille replied. "We're meeting my mom at the train station. She's taking you to the emergency room."

* * *

"The . . . e-emergency . . . room?" stammered Art. "We . . . I . . . We can't. We have to go to Westminster Abbey."

"No," replied Camille. "You're hurt."

"I'm fine," insisted Art.

"Your forearm is the size of a football," said Camille. "And you can barely move without looking like you're about to die."

"I'm fine," repeated Art, this time with much less conviction.

"You'd make me go to the doctor," said Camille.

Art paused. He turned and stared out the window. The rain was now coming down hard, blurring the landscape as it rushed by the train's window. His arm ached every time he moved. He knew she was right.

"What did you tell your mom?" Art asked.

"Just enough," she said. "That you hurt your arm at the Tower of London and that it might be broken. She kinda freaked — never even asked how it happened."

Art nodded. "She's going to want to know," he said. "And then what do we tell her?"

Broderick had just settled into his hotel room when his phone rang.

He picked it up. "Yes?" he said.

It was Miles Davenport. "I'll pick you up in front of the hotel at five thirty," he said.

Broderick Tinsley felt as if he had not slept or eaten in days. A good meal, a hot shower, and a solid night's sleep would have hit the spot. But he also knew that the sooner he made it to Westminster Abbey, the better.

It was almost over, he told himself.

"Okay," Broderick finally replied. "Five thirty outside."

Click. The line went dead.

CHAPTER 50

Camille and Art stepped off the train and into the vast confines of Paddington station. Dark gray clouds swirled above the train station's wide glass roof. Commuters hurried about in their suits and business attire, umbrellas at the ready. Weary parents chased after young children. Teenagers stood about, sipping coffee and complaining about the gathering storm. The sounds of footsteps, trains, and voices merged together into a low rumble that echoed back and forth throughout the massive space. Camille and Art made their way through the crowds and across the station. Camille spied her mom standing just inside the entrance.

"Uh-oh," Camille said.

"What?" Art asked.

"Full bear mode," Camille responded.

"What does that mean?" said Art.

"You'll see," Camille replied.

Mary Sullivan was typically levelheaded and rational. But when required, she could transition into full mother-bear mode—protective, focused, and intense. Camille had learned long ago that it was best to shut up in those situations and do what she was told.

"What happened?" Mary Sullivan demanded as soon as Art and Camille had made their way over to her. "Are you okay? Does it hurt? Is there any blood?"

"It's fine, Ms. Sullivan," Art said. "Really."

But Mary Sullivan wasn't buying it. "Let me see your arm," she insisted.

Art took off his cap and carefully removed the long-sleeved T-shirt that he had been wearing.

Mary Sullivan and Camille gasped. Camille had not actually seen Art's arm since they had arrived at the train station in Windsor. It looked terrible. Swollen from just above his wrist to his elbow, it had taken on a weird purple color.

Mary Sullivan didn't hesitate.

"Let's go," she said as she turned to head toward the exit. "St Mary's emergency room is just around the corner."

Art didn't budge. "I just need some ice," he insisted. "It'll be okay."

Uh-oh, thought Camille.

Mary Sullivan swung around.

"Not another word," she growled. "Understood?"

Art nodded. "Yes, ma'am."

Mary Sullivan turned and headed toward the exit. Art and Camille hurried to catch up with her. They exited from the station onto Praed Street and turned left. Mary Sullivan ignored the pounding rain and the crowds as she plowed her way down the sidewalk. They reached the entrance to the emergency room in fewer than four minutes. Mary Sullivan directed Art and Camille to a pair of chairs in the waiting room.

"Sit," she instructed.

Camille and Art watched as Mary Sullivan marched over to the admissions desk.

"Wow," said Art. "I've never seen your mother this intense."

Camille glanced down at Art's arm. "It looks pretty bad," she said.

A moment later Mary Sullivan reappeared with a clipboard and large stack of forms. "Come with me," she said to Art. "They're taking you to an examination room."

She looked at Camille. "Wait for us here," she instructed. "This is going to take a while."

Mary Sullivan did not wait for a response from Camille. She motioned Art toward a set of double doors at the far side of the waiting room. An orderly dressed in white scrubs was waiting for them.

Camille watched Art and her mother disappear though the doors. She knew that she had made the right decision. Art was not only the smartest person she knew, he was also tough and determined. He would have done anything he needed to do to help her father—broken arm or not. But

Art was in a lot of pain, and his arm was getting worse by the minute. He needed to see a doctor.

Camille glanced at the clock above the admissions desk.

She still had time.

She placed the call.

Voice mail.

She left a message and hoped that it would be enough.

Camille gathered her backpack and headed back into the rain.

CHAPTER 51

4:45 p.m.
Thursday, August 14
London, England

The faithful had worshiped and prayed on the grounds of Westminster Abbey for a thousand years—perhaps longer. Stonemasons Henry of Reyns, John of Gloucester, and Robert of Beverly had directed the initial construction of the current abbey in the thirteenth century. And although Henry, John, and Robert had been dead for centuries by the time the building was finally complete, their vision had remained largely intact. The abbey was a massive, thick, and imposing structure befitting its role in the history of England. The land on which the abbey rested had served as the place of coronation for British monarchs for almost a millennium. But it was not merely a grand testament to the monarchy. It was a testament to England itself. The oldest door in the entire kingdom rested within its walls—a door of thick wood planks and black iron that had been built more than a thousand years ago. And more than three thousand souls rested within the abbey's ancient tombs and stone floors, including many of the greatest figures in English history: Charles

Darwin, Stephen Hawking, Sir Isaac Newton, Geoffrey Chaucer, Charles Dickens, Rudyard Kipling, Elizabeth I, Mary Queen of Scots, James I, and countless other kings, queens, poets, authors, artists, scientists, and politicians. And, if the riddle on the hourglass proved true, something else rested within the abbey's walls.

Camille knew that she had to make it to the abbey that evening. She really had no choice—her father's life was at risk. The only chance she had was to find King Arthur's crown before he did. If her father and the large man found the crown first, she knew the thief would take the crown and dispose of her father. If she found the crown first, at least she had some leverage. Her mother, of course, would be furious that Camille had left the hospital. But Camille understood the consequences of her actions.

She had to try to do *something*.

Art had been right: using the Tube was easy. All she needed to know was a color and a direction. She'd taken the brown line east from Paddington station and then the gray line south. Camille emerged from the Westminster Tube station and pulled a small umbrella from her backpack. She knew from the map on her phone that directly above her was Big Ben. But the top of the famous clock tower was lost in the dark clouds. Across the River Thames she could see the lower half of the London Eye, the massive Ferris wheel that sat on the South Bank of the river. It was lit up in a brilliant blue. The sharp colors faded as the famed attraction rotated into the low clouds. In fact, the whole of the city seemed compressed by the darkening skies. It was late afternoon in the middle of the summer, but it felt as though night had already descended on the ancient city.

Camille could feel her heart pounding. She glanced back at the entrance to the Tube. She was in a strange city. She was only twelve years old. It would be easy enough to turn around and return to the emergency room. She might even make it back before her mom and Art knew she was gone. But she knew she couldn't. She would never forgive herself if she turned around now.

Camille took a deep breath. "You can do this," she told herself.

Camille checked the map on her phone and then made her way along Bridge Street until she reached Parliament Square. In front of her, directly across the square, stood the imposing north entrance into the abbey. A massive rose window gazed out from the façade like a giant, unblinking eyeball. Images of saints were carved into the stone directly above the massive wooden doors. The saints looked down from their lofty perches upon those who approached the abbey. Above the saints Camille could just make out the contorted faces of the stone gargoyles who stood guard over the church.

She made her way across Parliament Square and stood outside the low iron fence that surrounded the abbey. Dark rain clouds had settled along the top of the church, obscuring the roof, spires, and towers. Still, the abbey seemed impossibly large. It loomed above everything else.

Camille scanned the broad lawn and pathway leading to the abbey. The grounds were empty. She made her way along the fence to the western entrance of the church. The doors to the western entrance were open, but not for tourists. According to the sign outside the entrance, it was almost time for Evensong — a choral service held every evening at the abbey. Camille had read all about the service on the trip from the emergency room. Evensong was open to the public, but it was intended as quiet and reflective respite from the hustle and bustle of modern life. Camille did not feel particularly comfortable using the service as an excuse to get into the abbey, but what choice did she have?

She stared up at the imposing façade of the western entrance. Two towers — one on either side of the arched entranceway — reached into the low-hanging clouds. On the tower to her left was a massive clock — one giant gold hand and Roman numerals on a jet-black face. It was now 4:55 p.m. Evensong would start in five minutes.

Two men in red smocks stood beneath the arched

portal leading into the abbey. They remained close to the door to keep out of the rain. Small groups of men and women, hidden beneath umbrellas, approached the abbey. They placed their umbrellas to the side and quietly entered the church.

Camille anxiously scanned the small courtyard in front of the Great West Door. Perhaps her message had not been received.

She felt very much alone. Her feet were soaked, and her hands were shaking. Even though it was the middle of August, the temperature hovered in the midfifties. She was dressed for a day in the sun, not a rainy, cold, and overcast afternoon.

Camille took one last glance around the courtyard. She didn't recognize anyone. She sighed. She would have to do this by herself. Services would start soon, and she needed to get inside before they closed the doors. And even though she had no clue what she would do once she was inside, she knew she could not turn back.

CHAPTER 52

4:55 p.m.
Thursday, August 14
Westminster Abbey
London, England

Camille started across the small courtyard toward the western entrance. Suddenly a dark figure holding a wide black umbrella stepped in front of her.

"Why did you call me?" the dark figure asked.

Camille stared up at the face hidden in the shadows beneath the umbrella.

"I need your help with the final clue in the riddle," Camille said.

The tall, gray-haired woman looked down at Camille from beneath her umbrella. "So you've solved the first two lines?" Eunice said. "That's very impressive."

"Not if we don't solve the final one," said Camille. She took Eunice's hand and pulled her toward the entrance to the abbey.

"What's the hurry?" asked Eunice. "Couldn't we do this tomorrow when the abbey is open to tourists?"

"No," replied Camille. "I'll explain inside."

Camille and Eunice made their way over to the western

entrance. They were greeted by two men in red smocks. They reminded Camille of the stewards at St George's Chapel.

"Are you here for evening services?" asked one of the red-smocked men.

Eunice glanced at Camille.

"Yes," Camille replied.

The man smiled. "Excellent," he said. He pointed to an area outside the door where a number of umbrellas sat stacked against the wall. "Please leave your umbrellas over there," he said. "Services will be starting soon."

Camille and Eunice closed their umbrellas and placed them outside the entrance. They stepped through the large wooden door and into the nave of the abbey. Camille gasped. The abbey was unworldly—unlike anything she had ever encountered. St George's Chapel had been impressive, but it paled in comparison to the abbey.

The massive building seemed impossibly quiet and empty. Every step Camille took echoed through the interior of the vast church. Standing at the western end of the nave—the lights low, the ceiling dark, and the outside world shut off from her view—Camille thought the abbey was simply magnificent.

"First time at Evensong?" whispered Eunice.

Camille nodded. "Yes," she replied. "And first time at Westminster Abbey."

A man in a red smock waved at them from the nave.

"I believe he's trying to get our attention," said Eunice.

The red-smocked man pointed down the north aisle. "This way," he said politely.

Camille and Eunice started down the aisle.

"So why tonight?" asked Eunice. "Why the urgency?"

Camille stopped. "My father's in danger," she said.

"Danger?"

"Yes," replied Camille. "I don't have time to explain everything. But if we don't solve the riddle tonight, then something very bad is going to happen to him."

Camille's statement seemed to shock Eunice.

"The police," she said. "We must call them."

"The police won't believe me," Camille said. "At least not in enough time to help my dad."

Another man in a red smock at the end of the aisle motioned for them to continue walking. They made their way to the middle of the church — the crossing. Two groups of chairs had been set up in the crossing. Another man escorted them to an open pair of chairs on the far side and handed them a program. There were a hundred or so people seated in the crossing of the church. It was completely silent.

Eunice handed Camille her bulletin and a pen. She had written a question across the top.

What were the first two signs?

Camille scribbled two words: *sator* and *rotas*. She handed the bulletin back to Eunice. A moment later Eunice handed the bulletin back to Camille.

Tell them you need to go to the restroom. I'll meet you there.

Camille glanced over at Eunice, who simply stared straight ahead. Camille caught the attention of a young man as he escorted an elderly couple to their seats.

"Is there a restroom?" she whispered.

The young man nodded and pointed behind Camille. "That's Poets' Corner," he said. "On the far left is a small door that leads out to a courtyard. You'll see a sign outside directing you to the restrooms across the courtyard."

Camille thanked the young man and then quietly made her way toward the small wooden door. Poets' Corner — one of the most visited parts of Westminster Abbey — was unlit and shrouded in deep shadows. Camille, however, could still make out the grave of Charles Dickens. She passed through the door into a small enclosed courtyard. The rain was continuing to pour, and large puddles had formed throughout the courtyard. A small sign pointed to the restrooms.

Camille made her way around the edge of the courtyard to the restrooms and waited.

Several minutes passed. She could hear the voices of the choir within the abbey. The Evensong service had started.

What is Eunice up to? she wondered.

Camille checked her watch. It was now 5:05 p.m.

A moment later Eunice appeared at the door into the abbey. Camille made her way over to her.

"I know the answer to the riddle," said Eunice. "But what exactly are we looking for?"

"You won't believe me," Camille said.

"Try me," Eunice replied.

"King Arthur's crown," Camille said.

Camille waited for the inevitable expression of disbelief, but it didn't happen.

"The coronet," Eunice said matter-of-factly, as if everyone simply knew about the crown.

"You've heard of it?" Camille asked.

"Of course," Eunice replied. "It makes perfect sense."

CHAPTER 53

5:06 p.m.
Thursday, August 14
Westminster Abbey
London, England

"So what's the solution to the final line of the riddle?" Camille asked.

"I'll explain when we get there," said Eunice.

Get where? Camille wondered. Weren't they already where they were supposed to be?

Eunice turned back to the door leading into the abbey. She cracked the door ever so slightly and peered inside. Camille could hear the choir singing.

"No one's paying attention," Eunice said. "Follow me —and be quiet."

Eunice opened the door and stepped inside the abbey. Camille followed close behind and quietly pulled the door shut. The singing of the choir drowned out whatever sounds they may have made. Immediately to their left—almost hidden within the shadowy recesses of Poets' Corner—was a small wooden door.

Eunice eased the door open. "Go," she whispered to Camille.

Camille stepped inside, followed by Eunice, who pulled the door shut. It was pitch-black. The sounds of the choir were now muffled and distant.

"Where are we?" asked Camille.

Eunice pulled out her phone and turned it on. The light from the phone illuminated a narrow set of stone stairs leading up and into the darkness.

"We're inside the walls of the abbey," she said. "There are hidden passages throughout this building."

"Where are we going?" asked Camille.

"The triforium," replied Eunice.

Camille didn't know what a triforium was, but she did know what the prefix *tri* meant — "three."

Three windows at Wakefield Tower.

Three saints at St George's Chapel.

And now a "triforium" — whatever that was — at Westminster Abbey.

Eunice started up the steep and narrow stairway with Camille close behind. Camille could barely see more than a few feet ahead. As best as she could determine, they were inside the wall of Poets' Corner. After a minute or so of climbing stairs, Eunice made a sharp right turn. The stairs continued upward for several more feet, then stopped abruptly at a small arched wooden door. A sign on the door read TRIFORIUM.

Eunice pressed her ear to the door and listened. "Services should be over in a little more than a half hour," she said. "We'll have to wait."

Wait for what? thought Camille.

Eunice sat down on the small stone landing in front of the door. "And since we have some time," she said, "why don't you explain to me why you think Broderick is in danger."

Camille sat down beside Eunice and explained everything—finding the stolen hourglass and the riddle, the trip to the Tower of London, discovering Broderick in Wakefield Tower, Art's broken arm, uncovering the secret sign in the three windows, going to Windsor Castle, the Catherine Room and the three saints, the trip to the emergency room and sneaking away to Westminster Abbey. When she was finished, Eunice did not immediately respond.

"You're going to be in a lot of trouble when this is all over," she finally said.

"I know," said Camille. The realization of where she was and what she had done finally hit her. She was wet, exhausted, and cold. She was hiding in a narrow stone passageway in the walls of an ancient church with someone she barely knew. She had sneaked away from her mother, who was already frantic about Art's injury. Camille could only imagine what her mother's reaction would be when she realized her daughter was missing—again.

"You did it to save your father," said Eunice.

Camille nodded her head. She felt like crying. All of the emotions of the day came crashing down at once.

Eunice put her arm around Camille's shoulder. "Then let's save him," she said.

CHAPTER 54

5:45 p.m.
Thursday, August 14
Westminster Abbey
London, England

Camille wiped her eyes and tried to focus on the task at hand.

"What's a triforium?" she asked.

Eunice nodded. "If you look at the abbey from the inside," she said, "there are three levels. The bottom level is where we were sitting. At the top of the church are rows of large windows. That's the clerestory—literally the 'clear story.' But there is also a small level between the clerestory and bottom level. That's the triforium—a small, almost hidden space within the abbey."

Camille pictured the interior of the church in her head. "It seems like it's the second level, so why is it called the triforium?" Camille asked.

"No one's quite sure," replied Eunice. "Many older churches had only two levels—the aisle and the clerestory. As cathedral architecture developed, the triforium would have been the third level added. Also, because many early triforiums were crammed into the space between the aisle and the clerestory, they took on a triangular shape."

Camille nodded. "But why do you think we'll find what we're looking for in the triforium?"

Eunice did not reply to Camille's question. Instead, she put her ear back against the door. "The service is over," she said. "Let's head inside."

Eunice stood up and slowly opened the narrow wooden door. She held her finger to her lips and looked at Camille. "Quiet," she whispered.

Camille followed Eunice out of the dark passageway and into a narrow gallery of stone and thick wooden timbers. The gallery was completely empty. Not a single piece of furniture. Not a single monument. Not a single tomb. Immediately in front of her was a series of stone arches facing back into the abbey. Camille tiptoed across and looked down over the edge. She had not realized how high they had climbed. The view was spectacular. She could see down the entire length of the church.

Camille stepped back from the edge. That's when she noticed a single word engraved on a rectangular piece of stone between the arches to her left and right: *fidelis*.

Camille glanced at the next set of arches. Another rectangular stone, another word: *gratia*.

More Latin?

That couldn't be a coincidence, could it?

Camille could see similar rectangles between each of the arches in the triforium — each engraved with a different word.

Camille turned and looked around. Along the exterior wall were thick stone columns — the bones of the abbey that held the great structure in place. Between the massive columns and set into the thick stone wall of the exterior of the abbey were large round windows, each window at least twice her height. She remembered how small the windows had looked from the ground below. She walked over and looked out one of the windows at the London skyline. She put her hand against the cool glass. She could feel the rain pinging against the ancient window.

"You asked me why I thought we would find what we're looking for in the triforium," said Eunice. She had moved down the gallery and now stood near one of the arches facing into the interior of the church. The dim light from the large windows illuminated her gray hair and the wrinkles in her face. "What's the final line of the riddle?" she asked.

"O'er ye heavens youth was crowned," recited Camille from memory, "ye signs reveal what time hath bound."

Eunice beckoned for Camille to come over. She pointed to the floor directly below the archway.

Camille made her way over to the archway and stared

down into the abbey. She couldn't believe what she was seeing.

"No way!" she exclaimed as she gazed down upon the heavens.

CHAPTER 55

5:51 p.m.
Thursday, August 14
Westminster Abbey
London, England

Camille stared down at the floor of the abbey.

Below her were stars and globes swirling about in brilliant golds, greens, blues, and reds.

"That's the Cosmati pavement," said Eunice. "It's more than seven hundred years old. It represents the universe — the heavens. And it is the exact spot on which Henry VI was crowned King of England."

"That's a mosaic, isn't it?" Camille said. "My mom decorated a birdbath in our backyard with small pieces of glass. She made a sunflower. At least she said it was a sunflower. It was kinda hard to tell."

"It's sort of a mosaic," Eunice replied. "But it's made of stone cut into different shapes, not individual squares of glass."

"It must have taken forever," Camille said. She remembered how long it had taken her mother to put each individual piece of glass into place, and she had made only one flower.

"I suspect it did," Eunice replied.

Camille stepped back and looked around. "So we're here," she said. "'O'er ye heavens youth was crowned.' The crown is hidden in here — in the triforium?"

Camille paused. They had reached the final part of the riddle: *ye signs reveal what time hath bound.*

"And you know what the signs mean, don't you?" Camille finally said.

"I do," said Eunice. "And so will my son."

"Your *son?*" Camille asked.

It took Camille a full minute to process what Eunice had just said. It felt as if the air had been pushed out of her all at once.

"Yes," Eunice replied. "Broderick Tinsley is my son."

"That . . . that m-means you're my . . ." Camille stammered.

"Your grandmother," Eunice said.

6:30 p.m.
Thursday, August 14
Great Smith Street
London, England

Broderick sat in the car and stared out the window. Fewer than five hundred feet away was one of the greatest architectural structures in the world: Westminster Abbey. He had visited the abbey on hundreds of occasions. His mother had taken him there frequently as a child. He had drifted about the abbey for hours as a teenager. As an adult, he had spent days holed up in the Abbey Library poring over ancient books and records. He knew the keeper of the muniments and head of the Abbey Collection on a first-name basis.

He revered the abbey.

And now he was about to break into it — albeit against his will.

Miles Davenport had picked him up at the hotel about an hour ago. They had driven in silence and parked the car near the back of the abbey's gift shop. Broderick knew that their undertaking could not be accomplished while the abbey was filled with tourists, but Davenport had not explained how they were getting into the ancient building after it had closed for the evening.

They sat in the rain for another five or ten minutes, and then, suddenly, from the back door of the gift shop, a small light flashed on and off.

Davenport glanced around to make sure they were alone. The street and alleyway were empty.

"Let's go," said Davenport. He exited the car and headed toward the back of the gift shop. Broderick gathered his bag and followed.

When they reached the back of the shop, they found the door ajar.

Broderick was tempted to ask how Davenport had

arranged this, but he decided that it was a question best left unasked. Broderick stepped inside. Davenport followed and pulled the door shut. They were standing in the storage room of the gift shop. The exit sign above the door provided a small amount of illumination. Broderick reached into his bag and pulled out a flashlight.

"No flashlights," said Davenport. "They attract attention."

Broderick put the flashlight back into his bag.

"Do you know where you're going?" Davenport asked.

"Yes," Broderick replied as he headed into the gift shop. Near the back of the shop was a small door. A sign on it read THE CELLARIUM CAFÉ. Broderick opened the door and entered the room. The café was a modern addition to the abbey. It was constructed of birch, chrome, and glass—sleek and modern. It smelled of tea and shortbread. Broderick made his way across the café to an equally modern steel and glass door.

Broderick opened the door and turned to Miles Davenport.

"Welcome to the thirteenth century," Broderick said.

6:38 p.m.
Thursday, August 14
St Mary's Hospital
London, England

They had called Art's father from the examination room. And while he was understandably concerned about his son, he also expressed confidence that Art was in good hands. The x-rays had revealed a small hairline fracture in Art's forearm, which had been quite a relief to Mary Sullivan, who had feared far worse. But the swelling caused by damage to the surrounding tissue would have to go down before Art could get a cast. He would wear a brace and a sling until then.

Art and Mary Sullivan thanked the doctor and made their way back to the waiting room. Art stepped through the door and scanned the room for Camille.

Nothing.

His heart immediately jumped in his chest.

Please tell me she didn't . . .

Mary Sullivan also noticed Camille's absence.

"Where's Camille?" she asked no one in particular.

She pulled out her phone and dialed Camille's number.

"Voice mail," she said. Art could hear the anxiety in her voice.

He didn't have a choice.

This wasn't going to be easy.

"I think I know where she is," said Art.

CHAPTER 56

6:39 p.m.
Thursday, August 14
Westminster Abbey
London, England

Broderick and Miles Davenport stepped out of the polished wood and bright steel of the modern café and onto an ancient walkway. The covered footpath encircled the cloister garden next to the abbey. Lights that hung along the interior wall illuminated the centuries-old stones that paved the walkway. The wind had picked up, and the rain blew sideways onto the path. Broderick had always been fascinated by the paving stones in the walkway. They were an odd assortment of different shapes, sizes, and colors — all rich with age, striking in contrast, and absolutely lacking in any uniformity. There were no sharp corners or right angles in the footpath. Everything was smooth and delicately curved by time and the relentless pounding of millions of feet over a thousand years.

The men made their way in silence along the walkway to a tall pair of wooden doors at the far end of the garden.

"Entrance to the abbey," Broderick whispered.

Davenport nodded. "I know," he said, and pointed at the bottom of the door on the right. A small stone at the base of the door had kept it from shutting. Broderick assumed that the rock's placement was not happenstance. He opened the door and kicked the rock down the walkway. It clinked along the stones and came to rest against the wall.

Broderick held the door open as Davenport stepped inside. He followed Davenport and then carefully pulled the heavy wooden door shut behind them. It closed with a dull thud.

Broderick stood just inside the entrance and, for a brief moment, surveyed his surroundings. He still found it difficult to comprehend where he was and what he was about to do. But he could worry about that later. Right now he had work to do. He took a deep breath. To his left was the nave of the church—the vast open space that greeted visitors who entered by way of the Great West Door. Directly in front of him was the quire—where the clergy and choir sat—blocked from view by a large wooden screen. To his right was the collection of monuments he was seeking—Poets' Corner. But first, another stop.

"This way," he said to Davenport.

* * *

The taxi sat hopelessly mired in a thick knot of traffic. But there was really no other choice. The rain outside was relentless, and walking to Westminster Abbey was out of the question. All in all, however, Art would have preferred to be stuck outside shivering in the rain.

"Did either of you even *think* about what you were doing?" Mary Sullivan asked for what seemed like the hundredth time.

Art knew better than to say it out loud, but they had known exactly what they were doing. He had just spent the past couple of minutes quickly explaining about the riddle on the hourglass and how Camille's father was in grave danger —that he was being forced to search for a crown that had been hidden centuries ago. And Art had explained where Camille was headed—Westminster Abbey—and why.

"Think," Mary Sullivan said. "Is there anyone whom Camille could have called for help?"

Good question.

"Cos Masters," Art said. "She's a professor at University College London. She's the one who let us into Professor Tinsley's house. But I don't think Camille has her phone number."

Art paused.

"I suppose," he finally said, "that she might have contacted the lady from the bookstore. She helped us with the riddle, and she gave Camille her phone number."

Mary Sullivan's head snapped around. "Bookstore?!" she exclaimed. "What lady? What was her name? What did she look like?"

Art was taken aback by the sudden barrage of questions.

"Eunice," Art said. "She knows Professor Tinsley."

Mary Sullivan did not immediately respond. She turned and looked out the window.

"She certainly does know Camille's father," she finally replied. "She's his mother."

Broderick and Miles Davenport made their way over to a stone platform in the middle of the abbey. Velvet ropes separated the platform from the rest of the church. Broderick stepped over the ropes, and Davenport followed. Davenport glanced down the long expanse of the church. Despite the pounding rain outside, it was incredibly quiet.

"This is the sacrarium," Broderick said. "The word's derived from Latin—it means 'sacred.' This is the very spot where the kings and queens of England have been crowned for centuries."

"So what?" said Davenport. He had little patience for history lessons.

Broderick ignored him. He pointed at the floor—at the brilliant mosaic beneath their feet.

It took a moment, but Davenport finally realized why they were standing on the sacrarium.

O'er ye heavens youth was crowned, ye signs reveal what time hath bound.

"The heavens," Davenport said.

Broderick nodded.

Davenport looked up. Broderick followed his gaze to the arched openings of the triforium that surrounded and looked down upon the sacrarium.

"How do we . . .?" Davenport asked.

"Follow me," Broderick replied. They stepped off the platform and headed down the western wall of the abbey to the far end of the south transept. To their right hung the monuments and plaques of Poets' Corner. In front of them was a small wooden door. Broderick opened the door and peered inside.

"We'll need a flashlight," Broderick said. "But don't worry. No one can see us in here."

Davenport peeked inside the open door. He could make out the beginning of a set of stone stairs that quickly ascended into complete darkness. He grunted his approval.

Broderick retrieved his flashlight and stepped inside the narrow stairway.

As Broderick started up the stairs, Davenport pulled the door shut behind him and trailed him, following the light from the professor's flashlight up the narrow stone stairway to a small landing. Broderick turned right and proceeded up several more stairs until they had reached another door. Broderick cut off the flashlight. It was pitch-black. Davenport could hear Broderick breathing in the dark. Ancient iron hinges creaked as Broderick slowly opened the door. A faint light drifted into the stairwell.

Broderick stepped out of the stairwell and into the open passageway beyond. Davenport followed. The arched openings he had seen from below were directly in front of him. The men could now stand and gaze down upon the heavens.

They had reached their final destination.

CHAPTER 57

6:45 p.m.
Thursday, August 14
Westminster Abbey
London, England

As soon as he had seen the second sign—the wheels at Windsor Castle—Broderick had known exactly what he was looking for and exactly where he would find it. The key to solving the riddle from the hourglass was far older than Davenport or most anyone would have realized—at least two thousand years old, perhaps older.

"You know what you're looking for?" asked Davenport.

Broderick nodded. He had actually been in the triforium before, on a visit arranged by the head of the Abbey Collection. The triforium was a stark contrast to the floor of the abbey below. Every inch of the abbey floor—the nave, quire, transepts, everything—seemed to be covered with some sort of monument, grave, plaque, decoration, or memorial. But the triforium was different. It was uncluttered by history. It was an empty vessel. The only ornamentation that Broderick had noticed on his prior visit had been rectangular pieces of stone between the arches, each engraved with a single Latin word central to the faith of the church: *fidelis, gratia, Christus, Deus, tenet.*

Broderick walked along the triforium and read each of the words.

He stopped in front of the final arch and looked down upon the pavement below. Stepping back, he looked at the rectangular piece of stone between the arches: *tenet.*

In its most basic form, a tenet is a belief or idea important to a group. In Latin it is the conjugated form of the verb *teneo* — to hold, to keep.

"Is this it?" asked Davenport. "How can you be sure?"

Broderick reached deep into his satchel and pulled out a piece of chalk.

He took the chalk and approached the word engraved between the arches.

T E N E T

He wrote a "T" and then an "E" above the letter *N* in the word and an "E" and then a "T" below the *N*.

$$
\begin{array}{ccccc}
 & & T & & \\
 & & E & & \\
T & E & N & E & T \\
 & & E & & \\
 & & T & &
\end{array}
$$

He stepped back from the arches and looked at Davenport.

"Neat trick," said Davenport sarcastically. "But where does that get us?"

"The first sign was a sower," said Broderick. "The Latin word for 'sower' is *sator*."

Broderick approached the stone once again with his chalk and wrote:

```
S   A   T   O   R
A       E
T   E   N   E   T
O       E
R       T
```

Davenport did not say anything. Broderick could sense that he was beginning to catch on.

"And then there was the second sign — or signs," said Broderick. "The wheels in the Catherine Room at Windsor Castle. The Latin word for 'wheels' is *rotas*."

He took his chalk once more in hand and wrote:

```
S   A   T   O   R
A       E       O
T   E   N   E   T
O       E       A
R   O   T   A   S
```

He stepped back, turned on his flashlight, and shone it directly on the stone.

"It's a Sator Square," said Broderick. "An ancient and

mysterious palindrome—words that read the same backwards and forward. The square is formed at its heart by three words—*sator, rotas,* and *tenet*. No one is quite sure what it means, but these same three words have been found on buildings in ancient Syria and buried in the ashes of Mount Vesuvius. This square has turned up in excavations in England, France, Italy, Portugal, and Sweden. It's at least two thousand years old."

Broderick pulled out a small pocketknife and approached the arches. He carefully ran the blade of the pocketknife across the top edge of the inscription. Halfway across, the knife hit a small indentation. Broderick pushed in the blade about a half inch and then pulled down and out. The inscribed stone—which had appeared flush with the surrounding archway—suddenly popped forward. Broderick caught it before it could hit the ground.

A large cavity appeared where the inscribed stone had once sat.

Clever, Broderick thought.

Broderick handed the flashlight and the inscribed stone to Davenport. He then thrust his hand into the dark cavity.

Nothing.

It was empty.

A sense of panic welled up in Broderick. Had he been wrong about the clues? Had he been wrong about the riddle? What would Davenport do when he realized that the object was not there?

No, Broderick thought. *I'm not wrong. It must be here some-where.*

He took a deep breath and felt around once again.

His hand touched upon an object, but it was not what he had expected.

Broderick took the object in his hand and withdrew his arm from the opening.

"Well?" asked Davenport. "Do you have it?"

Broderick held out his fist and slowly opened it.

Sitting on the palm of his hand was a thin gold neck-lace with an oddly shaped stone pendant. It was dark gray, rectangular in shape with the top left corner chipped off. Tiny symbols and letters covered the surface of the small trinket.

It was the Rosetta Stone.

CHAPTER 58

Broderick tried desperately to keep from smiling.

Actually, he wanted to laugh.

Somehow—someway—Camille had beat him to the lost treasure.

But Broderick knew that even a slight smile could get him—and Camille—killed. He took another deep breath and brought himself under control.

Davenport, for his part, still seemed stunned by the necklace he had taken from Broderick and now held in his hand. He turned over the small pendant and examined it carefully. He held the small gray object within an inch of his large face.

"Made in China," muttered Davenport. "It says 'Made in China.'"

Before Broderick could respond, Davenport seized him by the neck. The large man pushed the professor into an archway and up against the low iron railing. Broderick's torso dangled over the edge of the triforium, thirty feet above the stone floor of the abbey. Broderick instinctively wiggled his right foot between two of the iron rails.

With his free hand, Davenport held the small pendant in front of Broderick's face. "Where's the crown?" he demanded.

His voice echoed through the massive building.

"I don't know," Broderick said.

Davenport tightened his grip around Broderick's neck and pushed him farther over the edge of the triforium. His black eyes bored into Broderick.

"Where's the crown?" he repeated.

"I . . . don't . . . know where it is," Broderick gasped. His lungs screamed for air.

Camille had sent the text message to Eunice as soon as her father and the thief had entered the triforium.

She had then stood silently in the darkness and waited. Every now and then her phone would vibrate silently — another call or text from her mother. Camille did her best to ignore them.

She could now hear Broderick's voice and his labored breathing. She could hear him protesting that he didn't know where the crown was.

She knew he was protecting her.

Camille checked her phone to make sure the message had been delivered.

It had been.

Help would arrive shortly.

But shortly might not be soon enough.

It had taken Camille several moments to recover from the shocking news that Eunice was her grandmother. And although a million questions had started swirling through her head, Camille knew that the time for questions would have to wait—they first had to find the crown. Once Eunice explained the concept of the Sator Square to Camille, everything fell into place. The signs—the word from the stained glass at the Tower of London and the wheels painted on the wall at Windsor Castle—had led them to the small, loose inscribed stone and the secret bound up in the hourglass. The crown was as simple as her father had told her—little more than a ring of iron. But the thought that it may have once been worn by an ancient king—a king who would later become known as the King Arthur of myth—made it seem heavier and far more important than its small size and lack of ornamentation suggested. Camille had carefully tucked it into a pocket in her jacket for safe-keeping.

Once the crown had been located, Eunice insisted on going for help. The gravity of what they had done and where they were seemed to hit her all at once.

Camille, however, had insisted that they couldn't go

for help until *after* Broderick had arrived. The presence of a bunch of police and abbey officials could surely force the man holding Broderick hostage to hurt—or—kill him.

"We might never see my dad again," Camille had argued. "This is our only chance."

This realization caused Eunice to agree, albeit reluctantly.

"So what do we do?" she asked.

Camille had explained her plan. She would stay behind in the triforium—hidden in the shadows—and await Broderick's arrival. Eunice would wait outside—far enough away from the abbey that she would not risk being seen. Once Broderick had arrived, Camille would text Eunice, who would then call for the police.

Eunice had agreed to the plan but had insisted that it was too dangerous to leave Camille alone in the triforium. She told Camille that they would reverse roles—Eunice would remain behind, and Camille would go for help. But Camille had questioned whether the police—or anyone, for that matter—would take her seriously if she tried to explain that her father was being forced to break into Westminster Abbey to find King Arthur's crown and that her grandmother was waiting for him in the triforium.

Again, Eunice was forced to pause and consider what Camille had said.

Eunice reluctantly agreed that Camille was probably right, and Eunice promised to summon help as soon as she received the text message. Before she departed, she made Camille promise to remain hidden.

Camille had promised she would.

But the circumstances had changed.

Camille had not expected the situation—the violent reaction to her pendant—to escalate so quickly, and it would still be at least several minutes before help would arrive. Art had been right—the large man with the mustache would do anything to find the crown.

One thing was clear—time was running out for her father.

Camille glanced around the corner, careful to remain in the deep shadows. She could see the large man holding her father over the edge of the triforium.

There were no longer any options. Promise or no promise, she couldn't sit back and wait. Something had to be done. She reached into her jacket pocket and placed her hand on the crown.

Camille stepped out of the darkness and into the dim light of the triforium.

"Let him go!" she yelled at the large man holding Broderick.

The man turned toward Camille.

"Give me the crown," the man said. His deep voice resonated down the stone passageway.

Camille made her way over to the edge of the triforium and pulled the crown from the pocket in her jacket.

"I'll drop it," she replied. "Let him go."

"Give me the crown," the man repeated. "Now."

Camille didn't budge. "Let him go," she repeated.

The large man nodded. "Fair enough," he said as he pushed Broderick Tinsley over the edge of the triforium.

CHAPTER 59

6:53 p.m.
Thursday, August 14
Westminster Abbey
London, England

"Metropolitan Police, how may I help you?"

"My daughter is breaking into Westminster Abbey," Mary Sullivan said from the back of the taxi.

There was a brief silence on the other end of the phone.

"Ma'am," the dispatch officer finally said, "would you mind repeating what you said?"

"My daughter is breaking into Westminster Abbey."

Pause.

"And how old is your daughter?"

"Twelve," replied Mary Sullivan.

Pause.

"And what, may I ask, leads you to believe that your daughter is breaking into Westminster Abbey?"

"It's complicated," Mary Sullivan replied. "You see, she's trying to save her dad, and there's this hourglass with a hidden riddle. Anyway, he's being forced to find King Arthur's crown hidden somewhere in the abbey, and my daughter is there trying to find it first."

Pause.

"King Arthur's crown?"

"Yes," Mary Sullivan replied.

"An hourglass?" the officer said.

"Exactly," said Mary Sullivan.

"A hidden riddle?"

"That's right," Mary Sullivan replied.

Pause.

"Ma'am?"

"Yes?"

"Have you been to the pub this evening?" the officer asked. "Perhaps enjoyed a pint or two?"

"I most certainly have not," replied Mary Sullivan.

CLICK.

Mary Sullivan stared at her phone.

"How rude!" she exclaimed. "He actually hung up on me! Can you believe that?"

Art did not say a word. He just nodded his head in agreement with anything that Mary Sullivan said.

Art knew that Mary Sullivan was at her wit's end. They were still sitting in the taxi and stuck in traffic. If anything, the rain was pouring harder than ever. She had tried calling and texting Camille but had not received any response. Art had helpfully suggested that Camille probably had turned off her phone or placed it on mute—she was, after all, breaking into Westminster Abbey. She couldn't have her phone going off at a time like that, could she? His helpful comment had elicited a withering stare from Mary Sullivan.

The awkward silence was broken by the ringing of Mary Sullivan's phone.

She looked down at the screen. "I don't recognize the number," she said.

Art knew exactly what Mary Sullivan was thinking: unexpected calls always seemed to bring bad news.

The phone rang once more before Mary Sullivan answered it. "Hello?" she said. There was uncertainty in her voice.

She paused and listened. The look on her face changed from anxious to angry.

"Didn't I tell you . . .?"

Another pause.

"I suppose you should have, shouldn't you," she said.

Another pause. Mary Sullivan looked out the window.

"Corner of St James's Street and King Street."

Pause.

"Just hurry, okay?"

Mary Sullivan ended the call and put her cell phone in her purse. She turned to the taxi driver.

"Drop us at the corner of King Street," she instructed the driver.

The taxi started making its way over to the side of the road.

"What was that about?" Art asked.

"That was the dispatch officer calling me back," she said.

"Why?" asked Art.

"Because," replied Mary Sullivan, "the Metropolitan Police just received another call about a break-in at Westminster Abbey—and it appears that a young girl may be involved. The police are sending a car to pick us up."

Uh-oh, Art thought.

What had Camille gotten herself into?

Eunice Tinsley paced back and forth in front of the iron gate facing the entrance to the north transept of the abbey.

The rain continued to beat down around her.

She could hear the sounds of sirens in the distance, but the traffic around the abbey remained thick and snarled.

She could barely believe the mess she had gotten herself into.

After leaving Camille alone in the triforium—a decision she had almost immediately regretted—she had made her way out of the abbey through a service door on the eastern end of the church and then headed north to Parliament Square. A large sculpture of Nelson Mandela stood at the southwestern corner of the square, the perfect location to keep an eye on the abbey and await Camille's text message.

She didn't have to wait long.

Eunice had barely settled in beneath the sculpture when her phone buzzed with a text from Camille.

Broderick had arrived. It was time.

Eunice's heart had started beating furiously. She had already planned what she would do, but her hand was shaking as she dialed the number. She placed a call to a friend—a retired detective with the City of London Police who frequently dropped by her bookstore—and quickly explained the situation. There had been a long pause on the other end of the line.

He must think I'm daft, she thought.

To her surprise, however, he took her seriously. Help was on the way, he had assured her. He told her to wait for the police to arrive. She had promised she would.

But help was taking too long.

She needed to do something more than just stand in the rain.

Camille stared in shock.

The large man had just pushed her father over the railing of the triforium.

She instinctively braced herself for the sound of Broderick hitting the stone floor of the abbey.

She knew there was no way he could survive a fall from this height.

All of her senses seemed to pause. She felt numb. She couldn't take her eyes off the dark empty space where her father had been just a moment ago. She had promised Eunice that she would stay in the shadows — that she wouldn't get involved.

But she had.

And now Broderick was almost certainly . . .

Alarm bells went off in the back of her head. A desperate sense of self-preservation kicked in.

Pay attention! something screamed from deep within her.

The reality of the situation hit her full force. The large man was now heading directly for her. And despite his enormous size, he was moving quickly.

Run! her brain screamed.

CHAPTER 60

6:54 p.m.
Thursday, August 14
Westminster Abbey
London, England

Camille turned and sprinted through the triforium. The interior of the abbey flashed between the open archways to her left. To her right were the large round windows that surrounded the triforium. She caught brief glimpses of the dark London skyline as she ran.

"Give it to me!" a deep voice behind her yelled.

Camille briefly considered dropping the crown and continuing to run.

Maybe the large man in pursuit of her would simply go away.

But that wasn't realistic. The man had just tossed Broderick to the floor of the abbey. There was no way he would leave Camille behind as a witness. She needed to buy time for the police to arrive.

She gripped the crown tightly and kept running.

The triforium passageway made a sudden turn to the right. Camille barely slowed as she turned the corner and continued to run. She could hear the footsteps behind her. The large man seemed to be falling back.

Moments later the triforium turned once again — this time to the left. The footsteps behind her fell farther and farther behind. The man yelled once more for her to stop, but the voice seemed distant. He seemed to be gasping for air just to get the words out of his mouth. There was no way he would catch her.

Directly ahead was another sharp turn to the left. Camille swept wide to the right to prepare for the turn. The distance between her and her pursuer grew larger with every step. Up ahead Camille could see the triforium turn back to the right.

She made the right turn and kept sprinting. She glanced to her left into the vast expanse of the church. There was still no sign of help. But it didn't matter. Help would eventually get there. She just needed time. Besides, the gap between her and her pursuer was growing larger by the moment.

And that's when the triforium came to an abrupt and unexpected end.

Broderick dangled backwards over the edge of the triforium. He looked down at the stone floor of the abbey far below. The only thing that prevented him from falling was his right foot, which remained hooked precariously around the iron railing. His foot was twisted into an impossible position, and his knee felt as if it was going to pop at any moment. He tried to block out the pain and focus on getting out of his current predicament. Camille was now alone in the abbey with Miles Davenport, and Broderick had no doubt what would happen if Davenport caught her.

Broderick took a deep breath and attempted to reach up and grab the railing. A bolt of pain shot through his leg. He fell back, his foot slipping farther up the iron railing.

Blood rushed to his head. It was getting harder to focus. He had to try again.

"Hello," a man's voice said.

Broderick looked up to find a portly man in a police officer's uniform staring down at him.

"That's quite a pickle you've found yourself in," said the officer. He reached down to grab Broderick's hand. "But no worries—she's already explained everything. Found me patrolling Parliament Square, she did. More officers are on their way."

'She'?

Had Camille escaped? How? Where was Davenport?

The police officer pulled Broderick up and helped him over the railing.

"Is she okay?" Broderick asked.

"Aye," replied the officer. "She's right 'ere."

Broderick looked past the police officer, expecting to see Camille.

Instead, an older woman stepped out of the shadows and stood beside the officer. It was a woman whom Broderick instantly recognized, but someone he never expected to find in the dark recesses of the triforium.

"Mom?!" exclaimed Broderick. "What are you doing here?"

"Trying to save you," said Eunice. "Where's Camille?"

"You've met Camille?" Broderick sounded shocked. "But . . . how?"

"I'll explain later," Eunice replied. "Where is she?"

Broderick pointed down the triforium in the direction in which Camille had taken off running. "He's chasing her," said Broderick. He offered no explanation as to exactly who was chasing Camille or what would happen if she was caught. The tone of his voice, however, was more than enough.

"I'm going after her," Broderick said to Eunice.

The triforium had come to a sudden dead end. Directly in front of Camille was a stone wall with a narrow wooden door. There was a brief moment of panic and confusion as she tried to make sense of what was happening. Her heart raced, and a million thoughts flashed through her mind. She had expected the triforium to run around the entire perimeter of the church. The unexpected appearance of the doorway had thrown her for a loop.

269

Calm down, she told herself. *It's just a doorway. It leads somewhere.*

But where?

And then, in a flash, she understood where she was — she had reached the western end of the church. She glanced over the edge of the triforium to the abbey floor. She could see the entrance to the abbey below her — the same doorway through which she had passed just more than an hour and a half ago with Eunice.

Camille now knew exactly what was behind the doorway in front of her: the clock tower. And if that was the case, then the stairs inside the clock tower would lead down to the floor of the abbey. She could be outside the abbey — and safely away from her pursuer — in less than a minute.

All of that sounded great, she realized, as long as the door would open. Otherwise, she was trapped.

Camille grabbed the iron handle on the door, turned it, and pulled. The door opened easily.

Camille let out a sigh of relief.

She glanced back over her shoulder. The large man had just turned the corner and was heading in her direction. But he was at the far end of the passageway — too far away to present a threat to her.

Camille stepped inside the clock tower and pulled the door shut.

CHAPTER 61

6:55 p.m.
Thursday, August 14
Westminster Abbey
London, England

It was pitch-black inside.

Camille pulled out her cell phone and turned on the flashlight.

What she saw almost made her heart stop.

The stairs leading down to the abbey floor were blocked by an iron gate. She rushed over to the gate. She could see the stone stairs winding down to the floor below. She tugged on the gate, which rattled but held firm. There was no way over, around, or under it. She took a quick inventory of her surroundings. A open set of stairs wound its way up into the tower. That meant she had to make a choice: go back into the triforium or go up.

The triforium was not an option. Camille could already hear the footsteps of her pursuer approaching. There was no way she could make it past him.

Her heart was beating furiously in her chest.

Going up, she realized, was her only choice — and it wasn't a good one. It was inevitably a dead end. But she needed to find some way to buy herself more time. Help, she told herself once more, was on its way.

She turned back to the door leading out to the triforium and quickly examined it. Perhaps it had a lock of some sort.

Yes!

At the bottom of the door Camille discovered a thick sliding bolt. She could see the hole in the floor that the bolt slid into. She bent down and tried to push the bolt into place. It didn't budge. She wondered how many years—or centuries—it had been since the lock had last been used. Camille stood up and brought the bottom of her foot down on top of the bolt. It didn't move.

She could hear the footsteps in the triforium. He was getting closer.

She pounded her foot once more on top of the bolt. It squeaked and edged downward ever so slightly.

The footsteps were closer.

She pounded her foot down again, and again, and again.

Camille looked at the bottom of the door. The bolt had moved—but not far enough. It was still a half inch from the hole in the stone floor.

The footsteps now sounded as if they were just outside the door.

It was too late to run up the stairs. She had to get the lock in place.

She pounded her heel down repeatedly on the bolt. Pain shot through her foot, but she ignored it.

Somewhere in the back of her mind she realized the footsteps had stopped.

She brought her heel down again, and again, and again.

C'mon, c'mon, she urged the stubborn bolt. *Move!*

Camille fell back onto the stone floor of the tower. Her right foot screamed with pain.

She looked up and saw the handle turning on the door. She stood up and leaned against the opposite wall of the tower.

There was nothing more she could do.

And then — unexpectedly — nothing.

The door didn't open.

Camille looked back down at the bottom of the door. She had managed to slide the bolt into place.

Her pursuer pounded on the door.

"Give me the crown!" the man demanded. He sounded furious.

CHAPTER 62

Camille quickly wound her way up the stairs until they came to an end at a small room. The floor was made of wide wood planks that creaked and groaned with every step. She could hear her pursuer pounding on the wooden door below. She knew it was only a matter of time before the ancient iron bolt gave way.

She needed to keep going. But how? The stairs had stopped. She knew the massive abbey clock was directly above her. She could hear the methodical grinding of its gears as it kept time—*THUNK, THUNK, THUNK.*

There has to be some way into the clock tower, she thought.

Camille scanned the walls with the light from her cell phone.

There!

An iron ladder was bolted to the wall on the far side of the room.

Camille ran over to the ladder and looked up. The light from her cell phone barely reached the ceiling. The metal ladder simply disappeared into a dark hole. She put her hand on the ladder. It vibrated with each turn of the massive gears of the clock.

THUNK, THUNK, THUNK.

Suddenly the light from her cell phone cut out. Camille glanced at the screen—black. The battery was dead.

Great, Camille thought, *just great.* Her only connection to the outside world was now gone. She put the phone into her pocket and started climbing toward the darkness.

THUNK, THUNK, THUNK.

Camille reached the top rung of the ladder and stretched her hand out into the hole. She felt the wooden floor and crawled onto it.

THUNK, THUNK, THUNK.

She could no longer hear the rain, the creaking of the floor, or her own footsteps. The sounds of the gears crowded out everything.

THUNK, THUNK, THUNK.

She took a deep breath and tried to calm herself.

THUNK, THUNK, THUNK.

She was now in the clock tower. Dim rays of light drifted into the room through small openings in the face of the massive clock. Camille's eyes slowly adjusted to the darkness. She could just make out the shapes of the large gears and motor that kept the clock hand turning hour after hour.

THUNK, THUNK, THUNK.

She briefly wondered whether anyone had ever been

caught in the massive gears of the clock. She clung close to the wall and started to make her way around the perimeter of the room. Perhaps there was somewhere she could hide and wait.

THUNK, THUNK, THUNK.

Nothing. There was no place to hide. Nowhere to go.

THUNK, THUNK, THUNK.

She continued along the perimeter of the room. Finally, in the dim light she saw something.

Is that a . . .?

THUNK, THUNK, THUNK.

A door?

THUNK, THUNK, THUNK.

Camille examined the small metal door. It was barely as tall as she was. The good news was that it did not appear to have a lock or require a key. A simple lever handle kept it shut. Camille could make out a small sign on the door. It read: AUTHORIZED PERSONNEL ONLY.

Well, it wouldn't be the first time she had ignored that type of warning.

She reached over to open the door and then stopped.

Something was wrong.

The room had suddenly turned silent. The gears had stopped moving. She could now hear the rain pounding on the tower and the wind howling outside.

"Nowhere to go," a deep voice said from the far side of the room.

CHAPTER 63

6:59 p.m.
Thursday, August 14
Westminster Abbey
London, England

Camille stood absolutely still. The wall of gears blocked her view, but she caught brief glimpses of light flickering across the ceiling on the far side of the room.

"Give me the crown," the deep voice demanded.

He was searching for her.

Camille watched the light move across the ceiling. He was heading in her direction.

"I know you're in here," the voice said.

Her only chance was the door. There was nowhere else she could go.

Camille reached over and took hold of the handle on the door.

She counted.

One.

Two.

Three.

She pulled down on the lever, opened the door, and stepped through it.

Camille recognized instantly that she had just made a huge mistake.

The police car pulled up next to the broad lawn on the north side of the abbey. The news that Eunice was Camille's grandmother still had Art spinning. He had a million questions, but those could come later. Right now they needed to help Camille.

Art exited the police car and looked around. He had hoped that the situation was not as bad as he had imagined. And he was right—it was worse. The police had set up a perimeter around the entire building. Art counted at least ten police cars, and he could hear more sirens approaching. And despite the pouring rain, the flashing lights had drawn a large crowd of onlookers.

A police officer handed Art and Mary Sullivan an umbrella and then led them across the lawn toward a group of officers huddled under the entrance to the abbey. It was obvious that whatever was happening in the abbey, it was serious.

As they approached the group of police officers, Art spotted a face that he immediately recognized.

"It's Eunice," he said to Mary Sullivan.

Mary Sullivan merely nodded and kept walking.

They reached the entrance to find Eunice explaining to the police officers and the abbey's head of security what had happened—and what was still happening—inside the abbey.

Eunice Tinsley turned to Art and Mary Sullivan. Her eyes were red. It was obvious she had been crying.

"Mary," Eunice said. "I . . . don't know what to say. Broderick didn't tell me about Camille until a few months ago, and now . . ."

Mary Sullivan did not immediately respond. She stood under the umbrella and just stared through the rain at Eunice.

This is going to be bad, Art thought.

Then suddenly, Mary Sullivan stepped out from under the umbrella, walked over, and hugged the older lady.

CHAPTER 64

7:01 p.m.
Thursday, August 14
Westminster Abbey
London, England

The rain was relentless. It drowned out the sounds of the city — the cars, the people, the rush of the river. It poured down her face.

Camille stood on a small porch just outside the clock tower door and assessed her options. Not one of them was good. She was trapped outside in the rain a hundred and fifty feet above the ground on a porch barely big enough to hold one person. Thick clouds and fog had settled over London and the abbey, and she could barely see more than a few feet in any direction. Above her she could just make out the bottom rung of a metal ladder that, presumably, ran up the side of the clock tower. But the rung of the ladder was too high for her to reach.

She realized there was only one way she could go.

Camille could feel her heart pounding in her chest as she edged herself over the short wall of the porch and let herself down onto the narrow stone ledge that ran along the exterior of the abbey. There was barely enough room for her to stand. She pressed her back as close to the stone wall as possible.

She yelled as loudly as she could into the distance, but her words were instantly drowned out by the rain and wind.

She knew she could not afford to panic—to make a mistake. Not now. Not on this rain-slicked, moss-covered ledge.

She edged a few more feet down the ledge until one of the stone gargoyles that lined the exterior of the abbey materialized from the clouds and blocked her path along the ledge. The massive stone monster glared out into the distance. It was so much bigger than she had ever imagined. The gargoyle served as a drain for the roof, and water spewed from its open mouth into the darkness below.

Camille was out of options. She knew that above her —far beyond her reach—was the copper roof of the abbey. Below her was a long drop to the stone path that skirted the ancient structure.

She was exhausted, tired beyond belief. The day's events fell on her all at once. The adrenaline rush was gone. She sat down on the ledge and scooted as close to the gargoyle as possible. She pulled her legs tight against her chest. The crown felt impossibly heavy in her coat pocket.

"Give it to me! Now!" a deep voice boomed.

Camille looked back at the small porch, no more than ten feet away. She could just make out the dark form of the man through the cloud, fog, and rain.

He was a real monster.

And she feared the real monster.

"Well?" Mary Sullivan said to the police officer. "What are you doing to help my daughter?"

The emotional reunion between Mary Sullivan and Eunice Tinsley had been placed on hold. There were more immediate concerns.

The question took the policeman off-guard. "You s-see . . ." he stammered, "we are working . . . organizing . . . quite . . . almost ready, you see."

Mary Sullivan stared at the police officer in disbelief. "Who's in charge?" she finally asked.

The policeman pointed to another officer standing just a few feet away. He appeared to be organizing a group of officers to head into the abbey.

Mary Sullivan marched through the pouring rain and over to the policeman in charge.

She tapped on the officer's shoulder. "Excuse me," she said, "but exactly when are you planning to go in there and find my daughter?"

The officer looked down at Mary Sullivan. "No need to worry," he said confidently. "We have the situation well under control. There is already have one officer in the abbey. We'll find your daughter and get her to safety in no time at all."

"You have nothing under control," insisted Mary Sullivan. "In fact, you need to—"

"Mary!" Eunice interrupted. She held up her cell phone. "It's a message from Broderick."

The police officer and Mary Sullivan turned to Eunice.

"Camille's trapped in the clock tower," Eunice said.

Mary Sullivan turned and looked up at the abbey. The top third of the clock tower was completely obscured by the low clouds. Whatever was happening in the tower was outside their view. She turned back to the police officer, who was likewise staring at the abbey.

"Well?" asked Mary Sullivan. "Are you going to just stand there, or are you going to go up and get her?"

Camille knew that stepping out on the ledge was a risk—particularly for someone of her pursuer's size.

"The crown! Now!" the large man demanded once again.

Her voice failed her. The wind blew the rain directly into her face. The clouds swirled along the edge of the abbey. Her breaths came in uneven gasps.

She reminded herself that Eunice had gone for help—that someone would surely be coming any minute to save her. That thought, however, no longer offered comfort. The cold water running down her right shoulder and the stone claw of the gargoyle digging into her back were stark reminders of her current circumstances.

An image of her father flashed through her mind.

She had failed to save him.

No. Not now. Camille pushed the thought aside. She could deal with that later — if there was a later.

Out of the corner of her eye she caught a flash of movement. The large man was moving — doing something. But the thick fog kept her from seeing exactly what was happening.

"Give me the crown!" the man yelled.

Camille looked in the direction of the man but did not respond.

There was more movement. The dark form was closer.

He was coming for her.

Broderick pulled himself up the ladder and into the clock tower. The police officer followed close behind.

The room was dark. The only noise was the unrelenting rain and wind.

"Camille!" Broderick yelled.

Nothing.

"Camille!" he yelled again.

Nothing.

"The clock's stopped," the officer said.

"Someone cut off the power," Broderick replied. "We need lights."

The policeman turned on his flashlight and started searching the room for a power switch.

"Where could they be?" Broderick asked.

The officer found the power switch and turned it on. The large gears started turning. The room hummed. The floor vibrated. Above the power switch was another, smaller switch. He flipped it on. Light filled the room.

THUNK, THUNK, THUNK.

"Nowhere else she could go!" the police officer screamed above the noise. "Except outside!"

THUNK, THUNK, THUNK.

Broderick's head snapped around. "Outside?" he said.

She wouldn't, would she?

Camille stared in disbelief. The large man had suddenly emerged from the fog. He was now standing on the ledge. Water poured down his face and over his thick mustache.

"Give it to me!" he yelled.

Camille shook her head.

She knew he could now reach her. There was nowhere else to go.

* * *

Broderick and the police officer were making their way around the clock gears when the officer suddenly stopped. He glanced down at his watch with a puzzled look on his face and then back at Broderick.

"They're late!" the policeman yelled.

"What are you talking about?" Broderick screamed above the unrelenting noise in the clock tower. "We have to keep going!"

The officer looked up at the ceiling with an alarmed look on his face. "Cover your ears!" he yelled.

"What?" said Broderick.

"COVER YOUR EARS! NOW!"

And that's when Broderick noticed it. Above the steady clack of the gears was a new sound—the sound of something winding up.

Broderick dropped to the floor and put his hands over his ears.

She wanted to look away. She wanted to close her eyes and pretend that she was at home in bed—warm and tucked under a thick pile of covers.

But she couldn't look away. Her situation wouldn't allow it. She was sitting on the ledge of an ancient church a hundred and fifty feet above the ground. Despite this, she felt almost claustrophobic. The world seemed to be closing in around her. The rain continued to pour, and the clouds swirled around her feet. And despite the fact that it was the middle of August, she was trembling and cold.

The large man stood on the ledge just a few feet away, staring down at her. She could see him testing the ledge —making sure it would hold the full bulk of his hefty frame. There was uncertainty in his movements but not in his eyes.

An odd thought occurred to her—she didn't even know his name. Not that it should matter. He had broken Art's arm, thrown her father from the triforium, and forced her out onto this narrow stone ledge. But then again, in some strange way, it did seem to matter to her. The term *thief* no longer seemed enough.

She took a deep breath and found the words.

"Who are you?" she asked. She was surprised by the strength in her voice.

He didn't respond.

She searched for any sign of pity or sympathy in his eyes but found none. He was concerned only about the small iron crown she held inside her jacket. He shuffled his feet ever so slightly, paused, and then reached out slowly with his massive right hand. It seemed to hover over her.

She resolved herself to close her eyes—and she did.

And that's when the stone monster roared.

CHAPTER 65

7:03 p.m.
Thursday, August 14
Westminster Abbey
London, England

The noise was overwhelming. Her eyes popped open and Camille looked around in panic. The narrow ledge vibrated beneath her, and she felt as if she was going to be shaken off at any moment. She reached up and grabbed the only object she could find—the stone gargoyle—and held tightly with her right hand.

Then she realized that the sound was not coming from the stone monster at her side—it was coming from the clock tower. The massive bells of the abbey were ringing. She could feel the sound in her bones.

She glanced to her left. The bells had also caught her pursuer off-guard. He had dropped to his knees, his massive frame now balanced precariously on the ledge. But his eyes betrayed no fear. Instead of retreating back to the safety of the porch, he started to inch his way slowly toward her.

She opened her mouth to cry out, but no words escaped.

The bells continued to ring.

He pulled himself down the ledge — one hand over the other, slow and methodical.

No! she wanted to scream. The ledge was far too narrow — wet and slick with the grit and grime of the city. He would never make it. And if he fell, he was certain to take her with him.

But he continued to crawl toward her, focused on the crown.

The bells continued to ring.

He was now within a foot of her. She watched him steady himself on his left hand. With his right arm he reached toward her.

She could see the thick mustache on his face, the creases around his eyes, the veins in his neck, and the water dripping down his forehead.

The bells continued to ring.

She tried to close her eyes once more, but her brain resisted.

And then, as she had feared, it happened.

His left hand slipped, and he collapsed to the stone ledge with a thud. The man's right arm flailed out in front of him and struck her in the ribs. She cried out in pain, and for a moment, she lost any sense of balance. She could feel herself slipping from her narrow stone perch. But her grip on the stone gargoyle remained tight, and she steadied herself. The crown remained zipped securely in her jacket pocket.

The large man appeared to have balanced himself once more. But she was wrong—his mass proved too great, the ledge too narrow, and gravity too strong. His legs slipped from the ledge—the rest of his body followed close behind. All Camille could do was watch. There was no help to offer and no help to give. He reached toward her even as his body dragged him down into the clouds.

The last thing she saw were his eyes—dark, empty.

The bells, she realized, had finally stopped ringing.

CHAPTER 66

7:04 p.m.
Thursday, August 14
Westminster Abbey
London, England

Camille stared down into the swirling clouds.

He was gone.

She felt lightheaded, exhausted. She just wanted to lie down on the ledge and fall asleep.

"Camille?"

She looked toward the porch. Her father's voice? He was alive. All she could do was stare at him.

"I'm fine," Broderick said, as if reading her thoughts.

She instinctively started to rise to her feet.

"Don't move," her father said. "Help's on the way."

"You're alive," she said out loud.

"I'm alive," he replied. "You're alive."

Camille nodded.

Out of the mist a bright light appeared. It floated in front of her for a moment, then slowly edged closer. As the light broke through the clouds, she could see that it was a spotlight attached to a large metal bucket at the end of a ladder. A fireman in a bright yellow helmet stood in the bucket and guided it toward her. He edged the bucket forward until it was directly beneath her feet. He reached up to her.

"Take my hand," he said, and she did.

He helped her into the bucket and then put a thick blanket over her shoulders.

"You're safe," the fireman said reassuringly.

CHAPTER 67

10:58 a.m.
Friday, August 15
London, England

Camille opened her eyes and glanced over at the small alarm clock on the nightstand in her hotel room.

It was almost eleven o'clock in the morning.

She rolled over and pulled the covers up over her head. She tried to go back to sleep, but her stomach was rumbling intensely. She needed to get up. There was a lot to discuss.

In a bit, she thought.

From the warmth and comfort of her bed, she found it hard to believe that just hours ago she had been trapped on a ledge high above the city of London. She had a vague memory of hearing her father and being rescued by a fireman. Everything after that was a blur. There were echoes of voices in her memory — her mother, Art, and Eunice. There had been flashing lights. She remembered crawling into bed. And there were other memories as well — memories of what had occurred on the ledge.

She tried once more to go back to sleep, but it was a

vain attempt. The hotel room was filled with light, and her mind was now racing.

Camille tossed her legs over the side of her bed and stood up.

Ouch.

Her foot throbbed with pain. She glanced down—it was wrapped in a large bandage.

"Good morning, sleepyhead," a voice said from across the room.

It was her mother. She was sitting at a small table by the window.

"Hot chocolate?" Mary Sullivan asked. "The milk's already warm."

"Are there marshmallows?" Camille asked. "The tiny ones?"

Her mother smiled. "Of course."

Mary Sullivan poured the steaming milk into a mug and stirred in a big spoonful of hot chocolate mix. She dropped in a handful of tiny marshmallows and offered the mug to Camille. Camille limped over and accepted the mug from her mother. She took a long sip and sat down at the opposite side of the table.

"Are you mad at me?" Camille asked.

Her mother pondered the question. "*Mad*'s not the right word," she finally replied. "I'm upset over what happened—I was absolutely scared to death. But . . . I understand why you did it, and you were very brave."

"But I'm still in trouble?"

"Oh, you better believe it," her mom replied. "You and Art are both grounded for the rest of the summer."

Camille sighed. Being grounded was becoming a way of life for her and Art.

"What about my dad?" Camille asked. "Is he okay?"

"He's fine," Mary Sullivan replied. "And I've extended our stay for a couple more days so you can spend some time with him."

The news caught Camille off-guard and the tears immediately started to flow down her face.

"Thank you, Mom," she said. "I didn't mean to scare you. I just wanted to meet him, that's all."

Mary Sullivan stood up and hugged her daughter. "I do understand how important it is for you to know your father."

She wiped the tears from Camille's face. "It won't be easy for either of you," she said. "He knows you have some tough questions for him. But something seems changed in him, and now he wants to be a part of your life—and that's not a bad start."

Camille nodded. She did have some tough questions for her father. It had been easy to avoid asking those questions in their short Skype conversations and in the middle of trying to solve an ancient riddle on an hourglass. But she knew that until she asked those questions, they could not really have a relationship. Still, thanks to her mom, the next two days would give Camille time to do what she needed to do.

Eunice! She had almost completely forgotten about Eunice.

"You won't believe this," Camille said excitedly, "but I met this lady named Eunice. She's actually my —"

"Grandmother," Mary Sullivan finished. "I know. And she's very excited about getting to know you."

"But I'm still grounded?" Camille asked.

"Yep," Mary Sullivan replied. "And if you don't mind, let's try to make it through the next year without being kidnapped, chased by criminals, or found on high ledges in the rain, okay?"

Camille smiled. "I promise."

A knock on the door interrupted their discussion.

"Is she up yet?" a voice on the other side of the door asked.

Art.

Camille hopped across the room and flung open the door. Art stood in the hallway, his right arm in a sling. Camille ignored Art's injured arm and gave her friend a big hug.

"Ouch," Art replied, but Camille could feel him hugging her back with his free arm just as tightly as she was hugging him.

"That was a pretty stupid thing you did," Art whispered in her ear.

"I know," Camille said. "I've been around Rat Hamilton too much."

She stepped back and held the door open for Art. "Hot chocolate?" she asked.

Mary Sullivan excused herself to make some phone calls, but Art suspected she just wanted to give him and Camille some time to talk — which he greatly appreciated.

"Are you okay?" Art asked. "I mean . . . you know . . . after what happened at the abbey?"

He had worried about her all night.

Camille took another long sip of hot chocolate. "I'm okay," she finally said.

Art didn't push it. He knew Camille would talk about what had happened when she was ready.

"I'm still confused about one thing," Camille said. "The steward at St George's Chapel said that the chapel was a Royal Peculiar — just like Westminster Abbey and the Tower of London. But I don't understand why that was important. I mean, I know now what a Royal Peculiar is, but why did the clues lead to those places? Why not some other castle or church? There had to be lots of other places where Henry VI did something."

It was clearly an effort by Camille to change the topic, but Art was just fine with that.

"I wondered about that too," Art said. "I asked

Eunice about it last night. The guy who owned the hour-glass—"

"John Dee," Camille interjected. "The wizard."

Art smiled. "Yes," he said, "the wizard. But he was also an advisor to Queen Elizabeth, so he would have had access to the Royal Peculiars. All of those buildings had been around for a long time before John Dee was born, and he probably believed they would be around for a long time after he died."

"So he picked places that he knew," Camille said. "Places that were safe. Places that weren't going anywhere, right?"

"Exactly," said Art.

"But why did he have to hide the crown?" she asked. "What was the big deal? It's just a rusty piece of metal."

Art nodded. He had also been surprised when he saw the crown. It was hard to believe such an unassuming object had led to such a dangerous undertaking. It had actually been Camille's father who had explained the significance of the crown to Art. "Queen Elizabeth did not have any children," Art said, "so there were plenty of people waiting to take her place as she got older. Arthur's crown was a symbol of true royalty, and John Dee was probably worried about how that symbol might be used—maybe even against the queen herself."

"So he hid it to protect the queen," Camille said. "I bet he didn't think it would stay hidden for more than five hundred years."

Art smiled. That was exactly what Camille's father had said.

Camille took another sip of hot chocolate and gazed out the window. She seemed lost in thought.

"Art?" she finally said. "Can I ask you something?"

"Sure," Art replied. He braced himself.

"Do you think we'll get to meet the queen again?" she asked. "Or Prince George? I'd love to meet Prince George. I mean, I like his parents also, but I think it would be so cool to meet George. If I had to put them in order, I would want to meet . . ."

Art settled back into his chair, drank his hot chocolate, and listened as Camille detailed all of the members of the royal family whom she would want to meet, her order of preference, and why she wanted to meet each of them.

AUTHOR'S NOTE

There is a tendency to think of art as simply paintings hanging in a museum. But art is so much more. This book includes paintings, but the story revolves around four very different art forms that are not found in museum exhibits — art that is part of a specific place and a specific time.

The first art form is architecture. St George's Chapel at Windsor Castle and Westminster Abbey are simply spectacular — not just because of their size, but because of the detail and thought that went into their construction. Each building was constructed without modern building tools and machines, and yet — incredibly — the peak of Westminster Abbey reaches 225 feet into the air. The buildings were constructed and decorated with stone carved by master masons. The stones were painted and gilded by hand. The structures are filled with symbolism. They inspire awe.

The second art form is stained glass — the careful construction of images through the placement of colored glass within a framework of lead strips. It is painstaking work that requires patience, practice, and dedication to the craft. In a time when literacy was a privilege of the rich and powerful, the stories told through stained glass were often one of the primary sources for religious instruction in the Middle Ages. And beyond instruction, they inspired faith. The magnificent rose windows at St George's and Windsor Castle are breathtaking.

The third art form is a mural, such as the wall paintings found in the cloisters at Windsor Castle. These paintings would have been known only to a select few. They were created to inspire confidence in those who had chosen to lead lives of service to the church and the crown. The murals would have served as constant reminders of the sufferings of those who came before them and the sacrifices made for their faith.

And the final art form is found in the floor of Westminster Abbey: the Cosmati pavement, a massive inlaid decoration of cut stone. This pavement is more than 750 years old, and yet the colors are as brilliant as ever. It contains a Latin inscription that predicts the end of the world, the translation reading in part as follows:

If the reader wisely considers all that is laid down, he will find here the end of the primum mobile; a hedge (lives for) three years, add dogs and horses and men, stags and ravens, eagles, enormous whales, the world: each one following triples the years of the one before.

But that is a mystery for another book.

The names of artists, artisans, laborers, stonemasons, glaziers, and mosaicists who created the artworks described in this book have largely been lost to history, but their creations—and hence their legacies—remain with us to this day.

Don't Miss More Lost Art Mysteries!

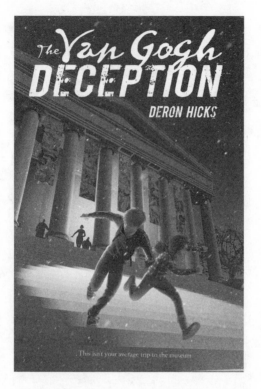

A Junior Library Guild Selection
A Sunshine State Young Readers Award nominee

★ "A suspenseful mystery romp with art
appreciation and a heartening trust in
readers' intelligence."
—*Kirkus Reviews*, starred review

"Readers will relish every surprise turnabout."
—*Wall Street Journal*

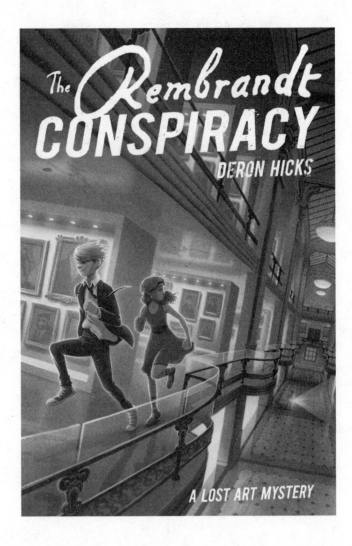

The Rembrandt CONSPIRACY

DERON HICKS

A LOST ART MYSTERY